To Tu[...]

Best

THE
ESSENCE
HUNTERS

CHRIS CONNAUGHTON

First published in Great Britain in 2019
by
Intext Publishing

A CIP Catalogue of this book is available from
the British Library

ISBN 978-0-9558707-9-8

Front cover images:
Shooting Star Studio/Shutterstock.com | IgorZh/Shutterstock.com
Shevchenko Andrey/Shutterstock.com

Cover design and layout by
www.chandlerbookdesign.com

Printed and bound by
CPI Group (UK) Ltd, Croydon, CR0 4YY

DEDICATION

This is for Caroline, with love as always.

About the Author

Chris Connaughton is an actor, writer and storyteller. He has worked in theatre, on TV and radio. Nowadays he is most often seen delivering his acclaimed storytelling shows to children, teachers and parents in school halls and arts centres all over the country.

His series of fantasy novels *The Beltheron Sequence* has been thrilling readers for over 10 years. Chris has also written plays for Theatre Hullabaloo and the Berry Theatre. At the moment he is writing a book of traditional tales for younger readers and is plotting a murder mystery novel.

To buy copies of the Beltheron books and find out more about Chris Connaughton's storytelling work in schools go to:

www.intextperformance.com

Acknowledgements

Well, this one took a while....

The Essence Hunters has been hiding away on my
ipad 'nearly finished' for about four years.
Each time I sat down to complete it, a commission
to write a new play or a suggestion for a different
project came my way.

Therefore the first people to thank are the ones who
made it difficult and slowed the whole process down
by offering me lots of lovely interesting things to work
on instead...

Firstly to Shonette Bason Wood, who involved me in
the creation of her Twist My Tales series of updated
fairytales and for which I was proud and happy to
be named as co-author.

To Justine, Peter and Ruth at Portsmouth Grammar
Junior School, for commissioning a lovely series of
storybooks for their pastoral curriculum.

And to Miranda Thain and all at the wonderful
Theatre Hullabaloo for approaching me with the
idea for writing Spirits of the Sea, a play which

demanded a very different writing voice. It led to great collaborations with Wayne Walker-Allen, whose music inspired lyric and poetry ideas which I could not have otherwise imagined, and with our director, Olivia Furber, who gave me a different focus on how I thought about and performed the words I had written.

Next are those who made it easy...

To Michelle Wallis who generously gave up her time to read and help edit the text. She offered valuable insights into themes and ideas which helped enormously in the final stages of writing.

To John Chandler and his team at Chandler Book Design for his striking images, professionalism and commitment to this project.

Most of all, and, as usual, my love and thanks to Caroline, who also helped edit, proof read, and, finally, convinced me to cut out at least half, if not more, of my commas.

Prologue

The animal on the table can't move. Its legs are tied down tightly with ropes. They run across the full length of the table and down to the floor where they have been fastened around metal rings in the ground. The creature's head is secured by an iron neck brace and a bridle that's screwed onto the table with thick bolts. A muzzle holds the animal's jaws wide open while the man works between its teeth.

The man holds a syringe in his hand. It is filled with a thick yellow liquid. A drop of it oozes out of the end of the needle.

'Hold still, pretty,' the man says. 'This won't hurt a bit.'

He reaches forwards, placing the syringe into the creature's mouth. It must know what's coming because it flinches, trying to pull its head back in spite of the bridle. It gives a whimper of fear.

'Hush, hush,' the man continues. 'All done in a moment. All over soon.' He purrs the words, as if he is trying to calm a frightened child woken from a nightmare.

His hand hovers for a moment, the needle against the gum of the creature. It whimpers again and then yelps sharply as the man pushes the needle further. His thumb presses down on the syringe.

When the syringe is empty, the man steps back. He looks down at the creature.

It lies there for a few moments, breathing heavily. Then it begins to writhe and shake. The fur on its hide starts to fall out in thick tufts, exposing pink skin underneath. The features of its face change too, and the claws at the end of its large paws become longer and softer. Within a minute it has altered completely from its previous shape, becoming a different creature entirely. It has shrunk in size until the tight ropes aren't holding it any more. If it tried, it could now shake them off easily.

It doesn't try though.

It doesn't move at all.

The man steps forwards again. He puts his hand onto the creature's neck, which is now a pale greyish pink. The man holds his fingers there for several seconds, feeling for a pulse.

He sighs and his shoulders slump.

A second figure steps out of the shadows at the edge of the room. He has watched everything.

'Well?' he asks.

'I'm sorry,' the man at the table replies. 'We've lost another one.'

'Were you any closer to success this time?'

The man gestures towards the dead creature on the table. 'The change is complete, as you can see. But so far we have not managed to ensure that any survive the shift.'

The second figure steps closer. He speaks softly. 'In that case,' he says, 'you had better try again.'

The Broken Jar

It was all the green sparrow's fault. If it hadn't flown so far into the thicket of bushes the boy would have got its essence by now. He could have been back on the path, and safely on his way home to the warm glow of the fire and his mother's home-made biscuits. Instead the boy was stuck between two spiny branches. He couldn't move any further forwards without the sharp spikes pricking through the front of his tunic. He couldn't back out of the thicket either because he could feel his right foot tangled up in a vine. It had somehow managed to wrap itself around his bootstrap.

The boy groaned about how he had got himself into this mess.

It had started last week. He had fallen far behind in his homework. His teacher was keeping a particularly close eye on him now. Any more mistakes and he might be thrown out of the essencing classes altogether. He needed to search for a good essence for tomorrow's class.

That's why he had set out early that morning. *'A feather would be good,'* he thought. *'Or a sloughed-off bit of lizard skin.'* Perhaps he could find some fur that had been caught on a branch from a passing pedjiaar, a big cat hunting for prey. Or maybe even a tooth! That would be a real find, and so useful for their studies in class. Feathers and fur could only be used once, but a hard tooth would last through several experiments. Even Vershan, his best friend, would be impressed if he came into class with a tooth.

He knew that other hunters would be out that day. Not only students from his own class, but professional essence hunters too, those who already worked in the high houses. He knew that the best chance of finding good material to work with, a pure essence from a wild creature, meant getting out into the fields first.

The sun had been smudging the tops of the rooftops as he tiptoed out of his house that morning. Even at this early hour his neighbours' dog, Beskar, had growled heavily from behind the door as he crept past. The growl ended in a single, threatening bark.

'Quiet Beskar,' the boy hissed. He tiptoed past. Beskar growled again. He always did.

If he could make a good impression in class tomorrow then he might be forgiven for his earlier failures. He might even get to go with his teacher, Cleve Harrow, to the essencing exhibition at the end of term. That was when he had the best chance of getting a job, to serve the mages and scientists who worked at the great halls and castles at the other side of Beltheron city. They were in the Cittegarre, close to the wealthy Variegatt houses. Yes, if he could find a good essence today he would show Cleve Harrow that he *was* worth something; he would show Vershan that he was the smartest after all, and he would show his mother that she had been right to let him become an essence student.

These dreams filled his head as he made his way down the scrappy Tenementerra alleys that morning. He had still been thinking about success as he walked to the eastern gate of the city and across the low grassy plain towards the thick trees of Beltheron forest. And he carried on thinking about it during a long, unsuccessful day, where he had no luck getting close to an animal until late afternoon. Then at last he had seen it. The small, bright green bird, hopping along the trail right in front of him. Success flared in his imagination again as he followed the green sparrow into the bushes.

He needed to catch the bird, to pluck a living feather from it, before releasing the bird back to the winds. A fresh, living feather was better than any old thing you picked up at the side of the road. That would give him a better chance of getting a job as an assistant to one of the mages of a Variegatt household.

His ambitions still swirling in his head, he crept further and further into the bushes. Now he imagined he was a quick and a silent hunter, forgetting it had taken him the best part of the day to find even a small bird. And even now the green sparrow still managed to keep out of reach.

It paused for a moment to peck at a seed-head on the tip of one of the branches, and the boy thought this was his best chance. He had a leather pouch fastened to the belt on his tunic. His essence collecting jar was safely wrapped inside it. Carefully, he reached into the bag to get it. In a moment the essence jar was in his hand, the stopper off and held between the boy's teeth. The sparrow was still pecking away, not concerned about how close he was getting. The boy reached forwards, perhaps a little bit too far, lost his balance and grabbed at a branch to stop himself falling. He felt the spike stab deep into his palm and jumped back sharply. The essence jar slipped from his other hand.

The boy's ambitions and daydreams disappeared as the jar shattered on the hard ground.

He gave a cry of anger and despair. He bent down to try to pick up the broken pieces. As he moved he felt the stab of more thorns across his arms. He was stuck.

The essence jars were valuable. Very valuable. You only got one. The boy knew just how important they were to the people of Beltheron. Young students like himself were presented with the highly polished glass bottles in a long serious ceremony. If you were clumsy or stupid enough to lose yours, or break it, then your family had to present the mages with payment for a replacement. He had once heard about how much this cost, and the thought made him grow pale. His mother could never afford even half so much. They only had a small cottage in the Tenementerra on the outskirts of the city. They barely had enough to keep paying the rent on that. His mother was always going on about how short of funds they were. She complained about him studying to be an essence hunter as well. The training lasted a full year and there was no time for him to take another job in the meantime. She grumbled about how it was a stupid idea and would never lead to anything. News of the broken jar would make it so much worse.

Cleve Harrow would be furious with him too. The Cleve had told him that he was quite a promising young student, but he was too absent-minded and he needed to focus much more closely on his lessons.

Perhaps he was better off staying where he was – stuck in this ridiculous position in the middle of the thorns and spikes. At least while he was here he wouldn't have to put up with any of their moans and complaints about him.

Even as he was thinking this, he heard a sound that changed his mind. Behind him, just over his left shoulder, there was a growl. It didn't sound angry - not yet - but it did sound like the sort of growl that said: *'This is my thorn bush. You have not been invited. You are in my way and I'm getting impatient.'*

The boy twisted slightly to try to see behind him. Even that small movement made him wince as another spike from the bush pierced his cheek. The growl behind him grew louder. And now it *was* angry.

He gulped hard. He still couldn't move his head enough

to see it. Could it be a pedjiaar? The thought of the big cats terrified him, but they didn't usually stray into this part of the forest. It was too near to the city walls. The boy realised it was more likely to be a silkefox, with their needle sharp teeth and avid hunger. Recently they had been seen more and more frequently. People had reported several sightings of silkefoxes lurking near to the refuse points at the edges of the city. Perhaps this was one of those?

Before he had time to think about this any further, the creature – whatever it was - gave a sniff and lurched off. He heard it running away through the undergrowth. The boy managed to turn his head just enough to see a flash of red and grey striped fur.

'So it *was* a pedjiaar,' he thought. The red and grey colouring was unmistakable.

As the footsteps of the pedjiaar faded away, another sound came to his ears. It started as a low rumbling but grew louder until he could make out individual hoofbeats on the ground. Several horses, coming fast and heavy. A chattering squawk erupted from the thicket where he was hiding. A flock of brightly coloured birds scattered into the sky. Last of all was the green sparrow that had led him into this mess in the first place. It flapped its wings lazily, calling out a mocking *'tsit, tsit,'* at him as it went.

The hoof beats were much closer now. Still wincing with pain from the spikes all around him, he lifted himself into a more upright position so that he could see over the top of the bushes.

A cloud of dust rose up on the edge of the hillside only metres away from the thicket. The boy saw a sudden burst of neighing, whinnying heads, eyes flashing, and long scrambling legs and hooves. A dozen or more horses and riders broke through the trees and onto the path directly opposite.

He heard the excited cries of men and women.

'Hold fast, he's getting away.'

'Blow the trumpet.'

'That way, you devils!'

'On, on, after it!'

They were almost past the thicket. The dust thrown up by the hooves was heavy in his throat and eyes. He thought they had missed him altogether. But then the last rider reined in and turned his steed sharply. It grunted a complaint before coming to a stamping, snorting, head-shaking stop. The rider looked down at him. The boy peered up but the sunlight was in his eyes. Even when the boy squinted he couldn't see any details of the rider's face. Then he moved and the boy guessed from his size that he was a young man; perhaps no more than a year or so older than himself.

'Hullo there. You're in a fix!!'

The accent was obviously from the west end of the city; the rider must live in one of the wealthy apartments ranged along the Cittegare walls.

The boy's heart fell. Moments ago he had been dreaming about working for people like this one day. That seemed impossible now. Perhaps his mother was right. Perhaps he was wasting his time. She was always warning him about the rich members of the Cittegare area. *They've no time for the likes of us,* she told him. *They'll cut you down soon as look at you. Get in their way and you'll regret it.*

He gulped. If he had been discovered by the wealthy Cittegare elite, then maybe his troubles were about to get much worse.

Alianna

'**H**old still a moment; we'll sort you out.'

The stranger turned in his saddle. He unslung a long slender horn from a strap across his shoulder. He put it to his lips and blew a sweet, piercing note. The sound floated away and echoed through the trees.

The stranger looked back down at the boy in the bushes.

'That'll bring the others back. You'll see. We'll have you out in a slice.'

The boy hoped that 'out in a slice' was a Cittegare phrase for 'really quickly' and that he wasn't going to find himself cut out of the thorns in slices by the cruel looking blade hanging from the rider's side. He didn't fancy being cut up like one of his mother's cakes.

Moments later there was another swirl of dust. He heard shouts and a whinnying sound. Horse spittle splashed his cheek as the thicket of bushes was surrounded by several of the other riders. Laughter stung at his ears as they realised the mess he was in. Voices came at him from all sides.

'Well, well Lord Matthien, what have you caught?'

'Is it that pedjiaar?'

'Is it a silkefox?'

'Hargh hargh! Have you caught a fish, Matthien?'

'Ha, even better! Look at this!'

The boy felt their eyes on him.

'Poor chap.'

'Is he stuck?'

'Stupid question, of course he's stuck.'

'Hargh, hargh!' The pompous laughter continued.

'Need a hand there, friend?'

'Look at the state of him. Covered in cuts.'

'It's the thorns of course.'

'Been there long, old chap?'

'The scent of his blood'll bring that pedjiaar back.'

'Well maybe we should leave him there and wait for it. He'll be perfect bait!'

More laughter followed, most of it cruel. The questions and comments came so thick and fast he had not been able to reply.

The young rider whom they had called Lord Matthien was dismounting.

'Don't be asses. Give me a hand.'

He threw his reins to a girl next to him. She leant across, grabbing them easily. The boy saw a flash of bright, laughing eyes filled with excitement. She looked about thirteen and rode a sleek thoroughbred horse. The horse was the colour of young chestnuts. Lord Matthien jumped down from his own steed and stepped carefully through the bushes towards him.

'So my friend, where are you from, eh?' he asked. 'The villages? Tenementerra side of the city?'

At last the boy found his voice.

'Yes sir, on the Tenementerra by the eastern walls sir.'

'Jolly good. Fruit picking for dinner?'

'Hunting, sir.'

There was another loud guffaw at this from a couple of the older riders.

'Hargh, hargh! Hunting he says!'

'Hunting, is it? Then where's his bally horse eh?'

'Run off. Back to the slum stables no doubt!'

'Got to be the slums, hasn't it? Only have to look at his jacket.'

'You won't see a proper hunting horse in the Tenementerra.'

'Not unless it's roasting on the spits!'

'Hargh, hargh, hargh!'

'Tenementerra delicacy, horseflesh. Lovely!'

'Hargh harr!'

'Quiet!' Lord Matthien said. He crouched down at the edge of the bush, looking at the problem the boy was in. He turned back towards his companions. 'Stop messing around. Don't be rude. Just hurry up and help me will you?'

The others looked embarrassed.

'Righto m'lord. Hold hard a moment and give us a chance.'

The older men hurried to get their feet from out of their stirrups. They swung their legs over the saddles and dropped to the ground. The boy could see that they were much less important than Matthien.

The young lord turned back to him and spoke again. 'What were you hunting for, my friend, and where is your weapon?'

'I don't have a weapon, sir. Essence hunting is what I meant, and I was just...'

'Essence hunting!' Matthien was obviously impressed at this. 'As a hobby, or are you a student?'

The boy grinned, in spite of his embarrassment. It was a compliment that this young lord thought that he might be wealthy enough to go out essence hunting just as a hobby to pass the time.

'No sir. It's not a hobby sir. I'm a student, well, more like an apprentice sir. I hope to work with the mages one day.'

That sounded much more impressive. But even as he said this he cursed himself for trying to show off.

'Good show! An essence student,' said Matthien. 'Always been interested in those ideas myself.'

Lord Matthien was already cutting a way through the thickest of the brambles. He winced himself a couple of times as the thorns stuck into his fingers. The two older men – who the boy now guessed were probably Matthien's servants – were also hacking at the surrounding shrubs to get closer to him.

'By the way, I'm Matthien. Lord Matthien from the Variegatt.'

The boy felt embarrassed again. The Variegatt was the most expensive part of the Cittegare. If this young lord lived *there* then he must be even more wealthy and powerful than he had first imagined.

'And you are?'

The boy's head was still spinning, so he didn't reply at first.

'You are?' Lord Matthien repeated.

'Stuck crown-top over backside, that's what he is,' joked another rider who had just arrived in the group. He was closer to Matthien's age than the other men. He reined in his steed and looked down with amusement.

'Jorian, be quiet! I have to put up with enough nonsense from Bargoth and Dross here. Get yourself down and be useful for a change.'

The newcomer just grinned again. It was clear that he was not a servant, but one of Matthien's friends. The boy realised that he must be from the Variegatt too. The cruel sneer on his face made it obvious that he had no intention of getting down to help.

'Why are you wasting your time, Matty? The lad'll get himself out soon enough.' He pointed impatiently back down the forest path. 'We don't want to lose the trail. We'll never catch the beast if you don't hurry up.'

Matthien looked troubled for a moment. The boy thought that he was going to change his mind, and not help him after all. But then the young lord came to a decision.

'It's probably too late to worry about catching the pedjiaar now anyway. It will probably still be around tomorrow. I've never seen one hanging around so much. We can always come out again in the morning.'

Jorian still hesitated. His horse snickered and stamped its foot, as eager as her master to be back on the chase.

'Leave or stay, Jorian,' said Matthien. 'Either way, I'm helping him.'

'No need to,' said Jorian. 'He's a Tenementerra urchin. They're good at helping themselves. Scavengers and thieves the lot of them.'

The boy felt his head grow hot with anger. 'Sir, I'm not a thie...'

'Hush, no need. Quiet Jorian! Don't talk about him like that. It's ill-mannered and does you no credit.'

Jorian sighed and turned towards the girl on the chestnut horse. 'Come on Alianna, let's leave him to his new friend.' He leant in close to speak to her more quietly. As he did he raised his hand to brush some pale hair from her cheek. She seemed undecided whether to follow or not.

'Go if you must,' Matthien said. 'We'll have him free in a moment anyway.'

The two men called Bargoth and Dross were pulling at the last of the creepers wrapped around his feet. He noticed they still had wide grins on their faces. They had carried on chopping away at the branches all the time they were speaking. Now most of the toughest branches had gone from the boy's legs and around his shoulders. He realised with relief that he could move freely without the stabbing spikes cutting into him any more.

'Good show, nearly there,' Matthien said. 'By the way, you still didn't tell me your name.'

'It's Darion, sir, Darion Melgardes.'

'How long have you been in here, Darion?'

'A few minutes before you arrived sir, that's all. I'm very grateful.'

'No need, no need. There! Now we have you.'

Matthien helped him to his feet. 'Come on now, my friend. Show willing!' Darion stood up. He winced with pain as the deepest cuts complained at the sudden movement.

He staggered slightly, still feeling off balance. The muscles in his left leg had taken most of his weight while he was stuck; he could feel them starting to cramp up.

'Is he alright?' Alianna asked. She had made no move to follow the young man called Jorian. He was now more impatient to get going than ever.

'Of course he's alright' Jorian replied. 'Those beggars are like cats. Always land on their feet.' He turned to the girl once more. 'Come on, Ali. I'm not waiting any longer.'

He turned his horse with a hard, jagged pull on the left rein and kicked its sides heavily to get it to trot. The horse gave a short whinny of pain.

'If you're not coming too, I'll see you at your parents' dinner this evening, Ali,' he shouted over his shoulder as he sped away, still kicking at his horse.

Darion saw Alianna drop her head to one side. There was a smile around the corners of her mouth. She caught his eye and he looked away quickly.

Matthien swept back up into his saddle in one easy movement. He looked down at the boy, noticing his thin arms and legs. His tunic was badly torn and of poor quality. Apart from a leather pouch hanging from his belt the boy carried no possessions with him. Matthien saw how he limped when he tried to stand, and noticed the loose leather flapping from one of his shoes.

Alianna leant towards Matthien 'We can't leave the lad like this,' she whispered. 'He's hurt. Look at the way he's limping. It will take him an hour or more to reach the city walls in that state. The sun will be going down by then and he might miss the curfew.'

Matthien hesitated. It would be awkward to take the boy with them. Even so, Alianna was right. It would be bad form to risk letting the boy be left outside the city gates. He couldn't be seen to do that – especially at the moment with the rumours of roving animals so near to the city. At night-time the creatures seemed to grow in confidence; silkefoxes, pedjiaar, even hurlions were now a regular threat. The curfew had been put in place a couple of months before, to make sure the people of Beltheron were safely inside before dark. Even so, several young people, their age and even younger, had gone missing in recent weeks.

Alianna spoke again. 'We *can't* leave him out here. You have a duty to help, Matthien.'

He looked at Alianna and his face softened. He turned back to the boy.

'You'll need a ride back I suppose?'

Darion began to stammer a reply. 'I'll be fine, sir, just need to...' he winced again as the cramping pain in his leg got worse. Was it worse than cramp? Had he sprained or even broken his ankle?

'Nonsense, you're exhausted and a couple of those scratches look nasty. Couldn't dream of leaving you here to walk back. Besides, Alianna's right. It'll be dark before you can make it on foot.' Matthien smiled widely at him. He leant down and dropped his arm towards Darion. He held his hand open to pull him up. 'Come on. Jump up. Old Zarak here can take two of us, can't you boy?'

It seemed the horse understood him, for it whinnied enthusiastically. It shook its head up and down, rattling the golden chains of its bridle. Darion had never seen such a beautiful horse. Obviously a thoroughbred from the finest stables, its coat gleamed and shone in the early evening light like polished bronze.

'Well, if you don't mind, sir.'

'Nothing to mind about, think no more of it, a gentleman has to help out a fellow.'

Darion managed to hide a grin at the pompous way that Matthien spoke. He stepped forwards and was about to let himself be pulled up behind Matthien when he suddenly remembered.

'Oh, excuse me a moment. I've forgotten something.'

He turned back to the thicket of thorny bushes. They had now been thoroughly hacked to pieces by the swords of the young lord and his friends.

'What's he up to?' said Bargoth.

'Get himself stuck again he will,' Dross replied.

'Brains not uppermost in the slums of the Tenementerra. Know what I mean, Dross?'

'Haargh, haargh!'

'Quiet!' said Matthien. The grins dropped away from their faces. Then, more quietly he added: 'Don't tease the fellow.'

But Darion didn't hear any of this. He was too busy looking for the broken pieces of his essence jar. Thankfully it was easy to reach them this time, with most of the vines and thorns around them now bent or broken by sword blows. He reached down and wrapped the three largest pieces of glass in the cloth bag from his belt. There were a couple of smaller shards, and the heavier base – unbroken in one large piece – still to gather up. He was just reaching for these when he felt someone close behind him.

'Can I help?'

It was the girl, Alianna. She had dismounted and was leaning into the thicket just by his shoulder. He felt clumsy all of a sudden, and nearly dropped the bag.

'May I?' She held out her hand to take it. 'You'll need both hands to reach those.' He caught a waft of perfume as she moved. It smelled of honeysuckle and spices.

'I... Um... Thank you.'

He blushed as he handed her the bag. 'Watch your fingers, those pieces are sharp.'

'What was it, a flask?'

'Essence jar.'

'I've heard of those, but I've never seen one. May I look?' She began to open the top of the bag.

'S'pose, yes.'

'Oh, what beautiful colours.'

He turned away from her as she looked at the broken glass. He felt his face burning. The thought of making such a fine young lady get down from her horse to scrabble in the dust was shameful. What would his mother say if she found out he had been so rude?

In another moment he had the final pieces carefully cupped in his hands. He turned back to her.

'I'd better put these in.'

She held the neck of the bag open for him as he placed the precious fragments inside.

'This glass, is it valuable?'

He nodded. 'Very. S'pose I'll have to try to fix it. I can't afford to buy anoth...' He blushed deeply again at this sudden confession of how poor he was. He looked down and saw the state of his muddy boots. The leather at one of the toes was curling up at the side. The stitching had come undone weeks ago. He had meant to fix it but had always put it off. Now it was too late.

'It's alright.' Alianna held out the bag to him. She smiled. 'Come on.'

He couldn't bring himself to look at her face, but he mumbled a quiet 'Thankyou, m'lady.'

'Huh, *m'lady*?' She pulled a face. 'None of that nonsense. Call me Alianna, or Ali, if you like.'

She stood and turned away from him. He caught another glimpse of her smile as she swung herself back up onto her horse.

'Ready?' asked Matthien.

Darion limped towards him and felt himself being pulled up onto the back of the saddle.

'Hold tight.'

Matthien clicked his tongue at his horse and it leapt forwards. The others followed close behind. He heard a whinny at his ear. He turned and saw a sea of bright golden hair curling in the wind as Alianna caught up with them. Along with the musty scent of the horses he caught another breath of honeysuckle and spice. Her chestnut mare galloped up neck to neck with Zarak. Together they spurred their horses on towards the city. He felt the throbbing of their hooves pounding deeply through his chest like his own heartbeat.

After a few seconds Darion heard the strident blast of a hunting horn. It cut through the noise of the galloping hooves and hung in the early evening air like a warning of fire or the threat of attack.

Matthien reined in Zarak to a halt. Darion had to grip more tightly with his legs to keep his balance. It sent another jolt of pain through his ankle. Alianna, Bargoth and Dross slowed down more gently up ahead. They pulled on the reins and circled their horses back towards them.

Matthien looked towards the line of trees they had just left. Darion followed his gaze, shielding his eyes against the low sun in the western sky.

'That's Jorian's horn,' said Bargoth.

Matthien nodded. 'Do you think he's found it?'

'Must have. He wouldn't call us back for anything less.'

Matthien hesitated for a moment.

Dross had also ridden up alongside. 'Should we go, sir?'

'We ought to,' replied Matthien. But he still waited, gazing towards the woods. Then he glanced up at the sun low in the western sky.

'We probably still have time before curfew.'

'And what about...' Bargoth jerked his head in Darion's direction.

Matthien nodded briefly and made his decision. 'Can't be helped,' he replied. 'You're up to it, Darion, aren't you? Can cope with a bit of a gallop, surely?'

'I, I think so.'

'But...' Bargoth still seemed doubtful.

'He can ride with me,' Alianna said. 'Your Zarak is swifter, Matthien, but my Hensa is stronger. She'll take both of us, won't you girl?'

Hensa, Alianna's chestnut horse, whickered and nodded her head up and down, excited by the thought of a race. Matthien's horse, Zarak, snorted as if to say; 'Think you're faster than me? You're on!'

The horn blew again.

'Lord, we are going anyway, with or without you,' Dross said.

Lord Matthien gave another quick nod. 'Right, off you go, we'll follow.'

Darion didn't have a chance to say whether he wanted to go with them or not. With an uncomfortable mixture of shoving, lifting and twisting, he found himself being moved from behind Matthien and over onto the back of Alianna's saddle. Bargoth and Dross were already racing away towards the trees. The hooves of their huge horses raised a cloud of dust, thickly filling the air behind them. Now, Darion heard another wail of the horn. Alianna clicked her tongue and Hensa leapt forwards. Darion's heart jumped in his chest once more as they sped after the other riders.

The Hunt

They galloped into the first group of trees. Branches whipped past Darion's face. He ducked and held onto Alianna's shoulders.

'Hold hard around my waist,' she shouted.

Gingerly, he put his arms around her middle. Immediately Hensa swerved to avoid a tree. The sudden movement almost spun him out of the saddle.

'Hold me tighter,' yelled Alianna.

He felt his face go hot again as he did what she said.

'That's better. Can't have you falling off. On, Hensa. Faster! Faster!'

The air was filled with shouts.

'To your left.'

'Ho there! HO! That way!'

'Follow on, follow!'

'Faster.'

'Into the river.'

'Hard at it now boys!'

'We have him, Sir! We have him!'

Alianna drove her heels into Hensa's sides and pulled sharply on the left rein. The horse gave a short grunt and swerved around a clump of shrubs and long grasses. Darion leant into the turn. His teeth clenched together in a grin at the sudden thrill of the chase.

'That's better,' said Alianna. 'Lean with me, and keep your head down.'

In spite of his excitement, his conscience suddenly stabbed at him. They were *really* hunting now. Not just essence hunting to take a feather or some fur; they were actually chasing down a living creature. The pedjiaar had scared him earlier, but he knew that he didn't want to see it killed.

'What happens when we find it?' he yelled through the rush of wind.

'We fire flares up. Scare it off. Chase it even further away. Make it unlikely to come back near the city.'

'Not kill it?'

She twisted back to look at him. She looked appalled.

'Lords no. Is that what you thought?'

'No. Good. I mean... I didn't want...'

He felt confused and couldn't explain himself. He didn't want her to think that he was expecting to see the animal killed. Or, worse still, that he *wanted* to. It didn't matter though. She was already focused on the track again.

'You'd better keep your head down.'

He looked on ahead and could see why. In front of them the trees grew more thickly. Low branches hung down over the track. The other riders were already rushing through. Darion had a glimpse of Matthien swinging down easily into his saddle until he was lying alongside Zarak's flanks. He only just avoided a branch that threatened to sweep him to the ground. Darion's stomach churned with fear and he thought he would be sick. He could never balance like that. He knew he would fall and be trampled.

'Down!' Alianna yelled again. In the same instant he felt her tilt right over just as Matthien had done, down to the right. Darion felt himself thrown off balance. In a jolt of terror he knew he was falling.

Too late to think about it, he just had to do as she said. Heart hammering, he dug his knees into the horse and copied her, lunging down to the side. Keeping one hand on the reins, Alianna reached behind with her other hand and gripped onto him. They were now both hanging sideways, almost horizontally, down near Hensa's galloping legs.

Leaves and twigs snapped past their heads as they raced on. For the second time that day he felt his skin cut by thorns and branches. He closed his eyes tightly and tried to shrink his head even further down into his shoulders, terrified of what was still ahead. With every hoof beat he felt himself jolted further and further out of the saddle. He let go of Alianna for an instant to grab onto Hensa's mane. This felt more secure, but he knew he couldn't hold on for much longer. In a blur he realised Alianna must be much stronger than she looked - and much stronger than he was. She was still holding on to him tightly with just one hand. It was as if she didn't even notice the effort, but already the muscles in his own arms were screaming at him to let go.

Then, in a final flurry of leaves, they were out of the snatching branches and into open space once more. Alianna quickly scrambled back into a secure position. Then he felt another hand on the back of his tunic and he was hoisted upright. Opening his eyes he saw Matthien galloping alongside them. It was he who had pulled him back into Hensa's saddle. He grinned at Darion.

'Great fun, eh?' he shouted into the wind.

Darion just nodded. He had no breath left to reply. Alianna spurred on Hensa to even greater speed. He heard her laugh with delight as they surged at full gallop, sweeping ahead of Matthien and Zarak. Zarak whinnied in dismay at being left behind.

Directly ahead of them the ground dipped away steeply. Even now the riders showed no sign of slowing down. If anything the horses seemed to go even faster as they plunged down the hillside towards the river below. Darion's teeth banged together as the horse's lurching movement down the steep slope threw his head backwards and forwards on his shoulders.

Bargoth and Dross were already in the water, their steeds splashing excitedly in the shallows.

Darion's sight was blurred and dizzy for a moment after the headlong jolting and shaking. He peered ahead and became aware of another rider on the far side of the river. The figure waved at them urgently. It was Jorian. He had ridden a little further upstream. Now he was near to a bend in the river. He held a long flare stick in his hand, ready to light.

'There, I can see it,' Alianna said.

Sure enough, on the far side of the bank only twenty or thirty metres away from Jorian, Darion saw the unmistakeable red and grey flash of the pedjiaar. As they slowed at the bottom of the slope he looked at it properly for the first time.

The creature was beautiful. Even in the fear and exhilaration of the chase the sight of it took his breath away. There was something majestic and noble about the way the pedjiaar turned its wide head towards them. The bright yellow eyes fixed on him for an instant as the big cat panted with exhaustion. He saw its striped sides going in and out as it breathed heavily.

The others had seen it too. With a jubilant shout Jorian pushed ahead into the middle of the river. One hand was still holding the flare. Then Jorian let go of the reins completely. He reached inside his tunic with his other hand. Darion guessed he was going to light the flare. He marvelled at how this boy, not much older than he was, managed to keep his balance on the horse just by gripping with his knees.

The pedjiaar gathered the last of its strength and leapt away.

Jorian grabbed the reins again and galloped after it, his flare still at the ready. Bargoth and Dross were close behind him. Darion lost sight of the riders as they rounded the bend in the river.

Alianna pulled her horse to a stop at the edge of the water.

'Too late,' she said. 'Jorian won't wait. He'll scare it off straight away, before we get there.'

Sure enough, a few seconds later Darion heard a fizzing, hissing sound shooting upwards. It was followed by a bright flash in the sky as the flare went off. It blinded him for a moment. He could understand how it would scare off any creature.

Zarak's heavy hooves splashed down into the river just behind them. Matthien was still gasping for breath after the chase.

'Did I miss him?'

'We all did. Jorian chased him off around the river bend.'

'Shame. Would have liked a closer look.'

Jorian and Dross were already riding back towards them.

'Success?' Matthien asked.

'Of course. What did you expect?' Jorian said. 'It won't bother us again. Bargoth is just making sure it's...'

'Gone for good with its tail between its legs, eh?' Matthien said quickly. 'Good, good. Well done, Jorian.' He turned towards Alianna. 'Come along. We had better get Darion back home.'

They turned their horses back up the hill and sped off towards the walls of the city that had just begun to glow with the fires of the early evening lanterns.

Home

As usual Beskar, the neighbour's dog, started growling at him as he approached his home. Darion could never turn the street corner before it sensed him, and started snarling. Its barking would grow louder and louder as he approached. Normally the dog made him nervous. Tonight he was too distracted to be bothered by it. He didn't even grumble his usual *'quiet Beskar!'* as he trudged past and opened his own door.

The interrogation began immediately.

'Where have you been?'

'Hunting, Mother.'

'Until this time?'

'Sorry.'

'Sorry is a word that comes too easily for you sometimes my boy.'

'But I...'

'And so is *'but'*. Look at the state of your face. All those cuts. Your hands too. What have you been up to? You're filthy with dust...and blood...and the lords know what else. Go and wash. Right now.'

He knew that arguing was useless. In any case he didn't want to get his mother into a worse mood than she was already. If he could, he wanted to avoid any sort of conversation with her. He didn't want to give her a chance to ask how his day had gone. He certainly didn't want her to ask to see what he had caught in his jar. If only he could get to his own room and hide the pieces away. Perhaps then he could find a way of fixing it before she noticed it was missing.

He made his way to the basin at the far side of the room. Their cottage had only three rooms; the main living, cooking, eating space, and two sleeping rooms at the back. The privies were outside behind a long wall, and were shared with four other cottages in their row. The wash basin was close to the curtain of his own sleeping room.

'I'll just put my things back here first,' he said as he ducked through the curtain. His mother wasn't listening though. He breathed a sigh of relief as he placed the cloth bag carefully under his bed frame. Kneeling down he pushed it right to the back, into the darkest corner he could reach. Straightening up, Darion pulled the blanket across the top of the bed so that it hung down to the floor, covering the bag even more.

He turned quickly and stepped back to the curtain. Pulling it slightly to one side he peered out, hoping against hope that his mother hadn't noticed anything strange about his behaviour. It struck him that she might be surprised at him actually tidying something away without being nagged first. He needn't have worried. She was still busying herself at the table, starting to ladle some thick vegetable broth into their bowls. It didn't look as if she had even noticed that he had gone out of the room.

'Hurry up and wash your hands. Supper's getting cold already and I've waited long enough for you today.'

Darion breathed a sigh of relief. She was thinking about supper, not about him. Perhaps he was going to get away with it after all.

After washing his hands in the bowl he came to help finish setting the table. His mother was still talking.

'I know I sometimes nag at you and go on. But I want the best for you Darion. You know I think so much about how you remind me of your father.'

How could he know that? She had *never* compared him to his father before! And he had never felt less like his father than he did now, skulking around, keeping secrets, scared of his own shadow. Her comments made him feel guilty. His father had been brave, confident, strong: the exact opposite of how he felt about himself.

'I want you to get on in this world Darion,' his mother continued. 'Your father was a respected man. A pulver guard that everyone liked. Working for some of the most important people in the city. We were doing well until he...'

Her voice fell away. She didn't need to say anything else. He knew what she was thinking about. His father had been killed while on duty. No one knew the exact details of what had happened that night, they said. But when his friends had brought his pale blue cloak to their door, the next morning, along with a medal for his bravery, they told them that he was last seen chasing an intruder from the Cittegarre gates, a bulky figure armed with several weapons intent on murder. His father's body had never been found, and at his funeral they had buried an empty coffin, covered by that same pale blue cloak.

Darion knew that he would never have such bravery. He could not challenge and chase an armed man. He daren't even speak up for himself properly in class, or even tell his mother about his clumsiness that day. The conversation over dinner turned to silence as he and his mother lost themselves in their own thoughts. It would soon be the first anniversary of his father's death. Perhaps that's what had been on his mother's mind. Maybe that was why she had started to speak to him like this.

As soon as things were tidied away he excused himself and hurried through the curtain back to his own room.

He took down his lantern from the shelf above his bed. Reaching for the matches sitting next to it in a little tray, he struck one of them against the rough edge of the bedpost. Guarding the flame with his cupped hand he lit the oily wick inside the lamp.

The glow grew quickly and filled his sleeping room with a warm, orange light. Placing the lantern on the table he returned to his curtain, making sure that it was closed properly. He knew that his mother wouldn't come in without asking – now that he was thirteen she was aware that he needed his own privacy – and so he dared to lift the bag from its hiding place under the bed.

With his heart hammering, he undid the cords. He paused for a moment before taking out the broken pieces. He listened carefully to the noises in the other room, wanting to make sure that his mother was getting ready for bed.

As he listened he heard her yawn and counted the heavy footsteps as she walked outside to the privies. From next door Beskar gave his usual deep growling bark. Darion started imagining what his neighbour's dog would do if he came up against a fully grown pedjiaar. That would shut up the stupid beast once and for all. He grinned at the thought.

Darion lay still and waited until he heard his mother return and move to her own bedchamber. There was the familiar *clack clack* of the curtain rings as she pulled the curtain roughly to one side. There was another sliding, clacking noise as it closed again behind her. Darion's shoulders dropped and he breathed out heavily. That was it for the night. If he was quiet now, she wouldn't come out of her room until morning. She did not mind his light burning. In spite of her many complaints against him she knew that he was a good student and that he would be studying his books. Even though she sometimes complained about his essence training, she knew it was probably his best chance of what she called *'getting on in this world'*. What's more, her mood had softened towards him tonight; so much that he still wondered at her change of attitude.

Darion took out the pieces of the broken essence jar. He placed the big, jagged chunks side by side on the bedcover. At least they hadn't smashed up any more while being shaken around during the hunt. But even so his heart sank. Now it came down to it, how *on earth* was he ever going to be able to fix it?

Darion held up a couple of the biggest pieces a little closer to the light. He noticed that the different colours of the jar formed a pattern down the sides. It looked as if the jar had broken along the lines which separated these colours. *'Perhaps they are weak points?'* he thought to himself. It occurred to him that the different lines of colour might disguise where he tried to stick it back together. *'If I can use some sticking oil along those lines and hold them in position I might get away with it.'* It was worth a try. He knew that tonight he had been lucky that his mother hadn't thought to ask him about his day's hunting. If she had he would have had to lie and he knew that never worked. Whenever he tried that with his mother the deep crimson flush of guilty embarrassment on his face always betrayed him. It would spread all over his cheeks and down his neck until the bright glow disappeared under his collar. No, it was always best not to try to lie to his mother.

Darion gave a deep sigh and started to put the pieces together. He kept a wooden box of oddments under his bed. Carefully, he pulled it out and began to rummage around it. He took his time so as not to make any noise as he searched. There were pencils and curled shells, some bits of strange rock he had collected, along with small tools; three metal screwdrivers of various sizes, a heavy wooden-handled mallet and a measuring tape made of real snakeskin. Finally, in the flickering light of his lamp he found what he was looking for. Tucked away at the bottom of the box was a small vial with a glass stopper. It was a bottle of sticking oil.

Darion twisted the top to open it. The familiar sickly smell of the sticking oil hit his nostrils. It made his eyes water.

He placed the vial on the floor and picked up two of the longest shards of the essence jar. He twisted and turned the fragments in his fingers, experimenting to see exactly how they might fit back together. Satisfied that they made a perfect join, with no tiny slivers missing, he put one piece back on the bed. Lifting the sticking oil again he tipped it slightly against the longest edge of the remaining piece. Using only a small drop of the oil, he spread it carefully with the stopper until it had covered the whole edge. He picked the second piece up again and tried to stop his fingers from shaking as he held the fragments together tightly.

It usually took three minutes for the sticking oil to set. He counted out the seconds under his breath. Then he waited for what seemed like another full minute just to make sure.

Holding his breath, Darion let go of one piece. To his great relief it didn't fall off. The two pieces remained firmly attached. He smiled to himself and moved on to the next piece.

Working as cautiously as he could, he continued sticking the various pieces back together.

Eventually he placed the repaired body of the essence jar onto the base. He had been lucky again, for there were still a couple of drops of oil left in the small vial. It was just enough to finish the job. As he held the final pieces together he moved it closer to the light. He wanted to get a better look at his handiwork. It seemed alright, he thought. Not perfect - you could still see the cracks in a few places - but if people didn't look too closely they probably wouldn't be noticed.

*   *   *   *

Even so he couldn't get to sleep. Too much had happened to him today. The pedjiaar, meeting Lord Matthien, the fast gallop on the horse and Alianna being so kind to him. It all swirled around in his head as he tried to relax. He kept rolling over in bed, trying to get comfortable, and wishing that his mind would just switch off.

Darion finally started to drift off into a dream of a horse with a long, swirling mane the colour of Alianna's hair. The horse began turning into a huge pedjiaar with a saddle of broken glass on its back when suddenly he sat bolt upright in bed. His adventures meant that he had not managed to collect any sort of essence all day. He would be far behind the rest of the class in his assignment and Cleve Harrow would be furious. Even though he had managed to fix the jar, he still faced a serious telling off the next morning.

'*Idiot!*' he said to himself. '*Did you really think that it would be so easy?*'

He tried to reassure himself there was nothing that he could do now anyway. He would just have to try to find an ordinary, old feather in the street on his way to class tomorrow. But the older, dead essences didn't work very well. And what if he couldn't find one in the morning? He knew he wouldn't have much time to search if he was going to get to his class on time.

Now he was completely awake again. He knew there was no hope of any more sleep. His anxieties about the next day were too much to bear. Silently, he swung his legs over the edge of the bed and got up. He needed to find some kind of fresh essence before morning.

He stepped slowly and silently to his curtain. At the same time his ears strained for any sound of movement from his mother's room. He could hear her low, steady breathing. Good. She was still asleep.

Darion picked his tunic and trousers from over the back of the chair and started to get dressed. It took twice as long as usual, each movement stretched out in silence. He realised that he had left his lamp burning, but now the wick had burnt so low that there was only the smallest guttering flicker of light coming from it. It didn't matter. It was enough for what he needed to do.

Picking up the essence jar he moved towards the curtain of his chamber. He didn't want the curtain rings to clatter together, so he stretched up and lifted his hand to the rail above his head to slide them back smoothly. Even so he held his breath until he had made a gap large enough for him to sneak through. He paused and looked back into his room. He wondered if he should have placed his pillow under the sheets and ruffled up the bedclothes. Then it would look as if he were still sleeping if his mother woke up and looked in on him. *'Too late now,'* he thought to himself, *'and anyway, there's too much risk of making a noise.'*

Stepping into the living area, he could still smell the remains of their supper. The smell stabbed at his heart. It was so comforting that he hesitated and wondered if he shouldn't just go back to bed and confess everything in the morning when his mother got up. He listened to her breathing. The rhythm hadn't changed. No. He had got this far, he might as well continue.

Off he went again, creeping towards the door.

When he got outside he moved more quickly. Thankfully Beskar must have been asleep in his kennel because he only gave a low, dreaming growl. Time was against him though. Darion needed to carry out his plan and get back into his bed before dawn.

Nighthunting

Darion crept towards the end of his street. He had an idea of which creature he was going to use for the essence jar.

The jars worked by placing an element of the creature inside – blood, fur, feather or saliva. The old mages who had first developed the transformation skill called these the 'essence' of the creature and it worked best if they were fresh. Once the essence was placed in the jar, a transforming liquid needed to be added. The liquid was created from the ground-up scales of the mutabar lizard and the oil of the euchar plant. The mutabars could live in the thickest forests, or on barren rocky outcrops. They could burrow into the earth, and even survive for long periods underwater. They thrived everywhere. There was no habitat in which these creatures could not live. That was what made the mutabar lizard unique. Once their ground up scales were added to the euchar oil and the essence you had put in the jar, they caused an elemental change creating a slimy mixture.

Drinking or sometimes even just sniffing this new mixture would then lend you the qualities of the creature whose essence you had transformed. A pedjiaar's fur would make you strong and brave for a while, a bird's feather would make you feel light as air and even able to float and soar off the ground for a few moments, and the scales of a fish would allow you to hold your breath underwater for minutes at a time.

Different mixes had to be made depending on the species of animal you used, and the age or size of the person the potion was intended for.

You had to be careful not to kill, or harm the creature you were hunting in any way. This is what made essence hunting so skilful. 'Any fool or cowardly brute can go out with a knife or arrows and kill,' Cleve Harrow had told them in one of the first lessons that Darion had attended. 'It takes no real talent to set a killing trap. An essence hunter must be more skilfull as they lay their snares.'

With tiny beasts like insects, you had to bathe the whole creature in the essence jar with the transforming mutabar liquid for a few moments, before releasing it again, unharmed. With larger creatures, mammals, birds or reptiles, a clump of fur, feathers or scales had to be washed in the liquid. It was then stored in the jar to be used when you needed it. The transforming liquid not only absorbed the qualities, or essences of the animal, it also preserved them for days at a time.

Harrow had shown them how to experiment with insects in class. 'See how swiftly they buzz around,' he had told them all. 'Their essence will allow you to move freely, changing direction as quickly as a thought, darting around objects and avoiding harm.'

The lesson was still clear in Darion's mind, and that is why he had decided to use an insect now.

Its fresh essence would give him the ability to move swiftly and silently around the class in the morning. It would be a great way to show that his jar was still working and Darion knew just where he was going to find one. He checked behind him once more. He was not being followed. There, in the moonlight, he saw what he was looking for.

The house at the end of his street had a small garden at the side. Tucked away at the back were a couple of beehives. The owner had let Darion see the bees at work and once he had been shown how to lift out the racks of honeycomb to gather the sticky honey.

Darion made his way to the side of the house. He could see the hives in the shadows at the back of the garden.

Darion crept closer. He lifted his hand towards the nearest hive and carefully lifted the wooden roof. Immediately there was a buzzing sound as the bees were disturbed. Putting the roof down on the grass, Darion took his essence jar and quickly opened the stopper. He took out a clean collecting stick from his pouch and gently teased one of the bees onto it. He placed it on top of the jar. The bee didn't seem to mind. Giving the stick a small shake, the bee dropped into the essence jar. In another moment he had pulled another small vial out of his pocket. The mutabar mixture. He unscrewed the top and moved it closer to the jar. This was something that he had practised many times. In one swift movement, the stopper was taken off and he added the liquid from the vial to the essence jar. Fastening the stopper he shook the essence jar gently so as not to harm the bee inside; one, two, three times. The bee and the liquid disappeared for a moment hidden by the smoke that now curled around inside the jar. The smoke solidified again until it formed a thick oil that settled along the bottom. The essence of the bee had reacted with the liquid in the correct way and he now had the potion that he needed. He was ready for his class in the morning. Opening the stopper once more, he was relieved to see the bee fly out again, quite unharmed. It buzzed its way back to the hive.

'*So far so good,*' he thought. '*Perfect result. If Cleve Harrow could see me, now, he'd give me top marks.*'

As long as the cracks in the jar held firm.

Vershan

T he next morning he checked the jar again before he even got out of bed. He had to make sure that it was still set properly. He knew that a number of secret elements were used in the construction of the jars – that was one of the things that made them so valuable – and he hoped that none of the qualities of these elements had reacted badly with the sticking oil overnight.

He held it between his fingers, carefully turning it this way and that, searching for any sign that would be noticed by Cleve Harrow. In broad daylight you didn't have to look too closely to see the cracks running around the jar. He groaned to himself. It had been foolish to think he could ever get away with this. But at least the sticking oil seemed to be holding. The jar still felt as solid as it had before, and as he ran his hands across the edges, nothing moved or gave way under his fingers. None of the oil from the bee that he had collected had leaked out either. This was all good news. He would just have to hope the Cleve didn't inspect the jars too closely while they were working.

He got out of bed and started to get ready for the day.

He toyed with the idea of trying out the liquid before he got to the college rooms. But he was interrupted by his mother's voice shattering the morning.

'Darion. Breakfast. Now.'

It sounded as if her friendlier mood of last night had gone again.

'Coming.'

He put the jar into his rucksack and carefully pushed it as far down as he could. Breathing heavily, his heart hammering, he went in to the living area to eat.

As soon as he sat down at the table he began to shovel down his breakfast. He was in such a hurry to get out of the house he couldn't taste the food. He stuffed his mother's salty pancakes into his mouth in one piece without even biting.

Darion ran from the house, surprising the sleeping Beskar, who raised his shaggy head and barked angrily as he sped past.

*   *   *   *

The road that led to the college buildings took him past his friend Vershan's house. Darion always stopped off to collect him on the way.

As soon as he saw him, his friend's mouth gaped open. 'What's happened to your face?'

Darion reached up to feel at the cuts on his cheeks and forehead. He couldn't help wincing. They had started to heal overnight but were still sore. 'Oh, nothing. I tripped yesterday, that's all.'

Vershan was clever enough to know that his friend was hiding something. The two boys had known each other ever since they were little. They had played together in the mud and dust outside the cottages, almost before either of them could even speak. Vershan felt that Darion was almost like a brother, and he could tell immediately that something was wrong.

'I will share your troubles for a story?' It was an old Belthronic saying. Vershan's father used it all the time.

Darion trudged on. He didn't answer at first. He knew he could trust Vershan but he was too nervous. Not only that, but what happened yesterday left him feeling embarrassed as well.

'Look, it can't be so bad if you're still walking,' Vershan added. It was another saying from his father.

Darion kept up his steady pace, not looking at his friend.

'You mustn't tell anyone,' he said.

'You know I won't.'

He stopped and turned to face Vershan.

'Swear it.'

'*Swear* it? It *is* serious then.'

Darion nodded. 'Please. Swear you won't say anything. To anyone.'

'Of course. But tell me on the way. We need to get a move on or we'll be late.'

They had almost reached the college buildings when Darion finished recounting his adventure of the day before.

Vershan's eyes had grown wider and wider as he listened to his friend tell him about yesterday's hunt, meeting the young members of the Variegatt and his problems with the broken essence jar.

'...and so that's that. I can't afford another, I daren't tell Mother, and if the bee's essence doesn't work in class today, Harrow will probably throw me out.'

As soon as Darion got to the end of his tale of worries though, Vershan's reply was simple and immediate.

'Share mine.'

'What?'

'Share mine. If yours doesn't work, then we'll just use my jar twice. If we're quick, no one will see.'

'Are you sure?'

'Why not, old Clever-Clever-Clevey is usually too busy to notice us anyway. We just have to make sure we get there early, so we can grab a desk at the back of the room.'

His friend seemed certain this simple plan would work. It made Darion feel better immediately. They picked up their pace and hurried on.

The shadows of the college buildings loomed up in front of them. Still whispering their plans to each other, Darion and Vershan hurried under the huge oak doors. They came into a shaded courtyard. It was at least thirty paces across, with a couple of granite paths crossing the lawns in the middle. There were dozens of other doors and gateways leading off it in every direction. A bell began to toll slowly. The boys heard it and both looked up at the bell tower. The deep clanging sound rang out again. Classes were about to begin!

'Come on,' Vershan said. 'Hurry up or all of the best desks will be taken.'

They ran across the courtyard to a doorway at the far end. There the two friends joined crowds of other students who were all hurrying to class.

Cleve Harrow

Cleve Harrow, their class teacher, stood at the desk at the far side of the room. He was busy talking to a young man. He had his back to the class and Darion couldn't see his face, but for some reason he looked familiar.

The back rows were already full. Darion groaned. He and Vershan managed to squeeze into places at desks half way down the class.

'Remember, don't worry if your essence doesn't seem to be working. As soon as I've finished the first experiment we'll swap jars and you just use mine again,' Vershan said. 'I'll already have the results to give Harrow if he asks me for an answer.'

'What if he asks me first?' asked Darion.

'I'll just answer anyway, pretend I thought he was talking to me,' said Vershan.

Darion nodded. It was such a simple solution. He had spent the best part of the night worrying, and Vershan was going to make it alright!

He looked towards the top of the class again. Harrow had finished speaking and the stranger turned around. Darion gasped. It was Matthien, the young Variegatt lord from yesterday. Darion's heart started hammering away at the sight of the newcomer, and he could feel his stomach begin to churn. Matthien must have seen the broken essence jar yesterday, and he was going to tell Harrow. His hopes were ruined before he had even begun the day!

'Students,' said Harrow. 'This is Lord Matthien. He has taken an interest in our work here. He would like to join us for this morning's class.'

Vershan nudged Darion's shoulder. 'Is that him?' he asked. 'Is that the same Matthien who rescued you from the thorns yesterday?'

Darion nodded and dropped his head down into his shoulders. He didn't want to be noticed by the young lord in front of the rest of his classmates.

It was too late. Matthien had already seen him. He waved across the room and gave a wide grin.

'There is my new friend,' he said. 'Cleve, would you allow us to sit together? He was so interesting yesterday, I would love him to tell me more about what you do here.'

'Maybe all isn't lost,' thought Darion. *'He* hasn't *come to tell on me after all.'*

'Of course my lord,' Harrow replied. 'Come down here boy. You will sit at the front with our esteemed guest and talk him through this morning's experiments. Bring your essence jar with you.'

Darion's heart sank again. He heard Vershan groan with frustration. Right at the front of the class! Harrow would be sure to see the cracks in the jar straight away.

'Sir,' said Vershan. 'He can't sir, the class is full.'

'Be quiet Vershan. That is not a problem. Melgardes can simply swap places with Bedellya here. She will have to sit next to you. Who knows? Maybe some of her knowledge will rub off on you.'

Vershan felt his cheeks burn as a giggle rippled around the rest of the class. It was no good. He had done his best but Darion couldn't refuse. After all, Matthien had just made a friendly request, and there was no reason why he shouldn't do what the Cleve had asked.

Darion moved forwards through the crowded classroom. The girl called Bedellya flashed an angry look at him as she stood up to swap places. Bedellya loved to sit at the front. Her hand was always up first, eager to answer anything the Cleve asked. She was smart, quick-witted and dedicated. Packing up her things, she grumbled to herself about having to sit with '*dull-headed Vershan.*' The giggles continued all around the class. Vershan's eyes rolled towards the ceiling.

Reluctantly, Darion slipped into his place next to Matthien. He managed a thin smile as his new friend grinned and held out his hand in greeting.

'Looks as if the worst of the damage has mended,' Matthien said as Darion sat down.

'What do you mean?' He clutched the cloth bag tightly to his chest.

'Your face,' Matthien pointed. 'The cuts are looking much cleaner today.'

'Oh! Yes, umm, much better, err, thanks,' he replied. He relaxed a little and released his grip on the bag.

'Bet they still sting though?'

Darion nodded. 'A bit.'

Harrow was already speaking to the class.

'You will all have completed your homework I am sure,' he began. 'So you should all have some essence already mixed with the transforming liquid, ready to experiment. We will examine your results starting with Darion here at the front.' Darion groaned. 'Afterwards,' the Cleve continued, 'we will show our guest, Lord Matthien, the effects of using *these* essences.' He gestured towards a row of fur and feathers spread out along his desk. 'We have the essence of a corvid bird, over here are the scales of a gourdfish, and...'

Before he could finish his instruction there was a sudden commotion behind them. The children all turned to look. Korellia, an eleven year old girl who always found it hard to concentrate on the experiments, had knocked her bag onto the ground. As Darion, Vershan and the rest watched, she rose slowly to her feet. One hand moved to cover her mouth, which was gaping open in shock. Vershan grinned and nudged Bedellya with his elbow. 'Korellia's having one of her visions again,' he said. Bedellya hissed at him not to be so cruel.

(It was well known that Korellia thought she was a seer, and frequently told people she could look into their futures, and even read what was in their minds. People – Vershan in particular - tended not to believe her.)

Whether or not Korellia really did have the gift of mind-reading and seering, she was obviously very disturbed by what she could see through the window. She stretched out a shaking finger, pointing to the courtyard beyond the classroom.

'B...b...brannoch,' she said. It was only just loud enough for people to hear, but even so that one word was enough to excite the whole class. Some leapt to their feet immediately. Vershan was already hurrying to the window. Others gasped in fear and turned to each other, not knowing what to do.

'Stay in your seats,' Harrow said. He had to raise his voice over the hubbub. Now everyone was talking. Brannoch were legendary. They struck terror into people's hearts. Luckily they were hardly ever seen inside the city.

Darion and Matthien looked at each other briefly. The young lord stood up.

'Pedjiaar yesterday, brannoch today,' Matthien said. 'Sorry Darion, I have to go. It seems I have another hunt on my hands.'

He moved quickly towards the door, only pausing to bow briefly to Harrow as he left. 'Cleve, my apologies. Some other time perhaps.'

Cleve Harrow waved him away. His thoughts were already fixed on the danger outside. He followed the students and dashed to the window. Vershan and two or three others already had their faces pressed tightly against the glass. 'Children, back in your places,' the Cleve demanded.

'There!' Vershan pointed excitedly. 'Korellia was right, it *is* a brannoch.'

'It's coming this way!' said Tarawen, the student standing next to him. Both of the boys ignored Harrow completely.

'Boys, come away from the glass,' Harrow continued. 'These creature are very...'

His words were cut off by a loud thump as something huge and heavy hit the window from outside. The brannoch had leapt towards them and now clung to the ledge outside. Vershan, Tarawen and the other boys leapt backwards, yelling with shock. One started crying.

Darion himself yelped in fear as he saw the creature for the first time. It was a dull grey colour, its skin wet and scaly. The body shape was similar to that of a human, but the arms ended in club-like hands with thick claws. Its head was blunt, like a gnarled tree stump. Its wide mouth gaped open, showing row upon row of sharp black teeth.

Darion took in all of these details in a second. Then the brannoch reached back with one of its arms and struck at the window a second time. It made a sickening thud. Everyone screamed out again. A long crack appeared down the full length of the glass.

Even with his attention fixed on the horrific creature outside, in the corner of his eye Darion noticed the Cleve moving swiftly. His teacher was now half way across the room. As he moved, the Cleve's hand reached into his cloak pocket. His other arm stretched out towards Vershan and Tarawen, who were still dangerously close to the window and the brannoch outside. The rest of the students had moved back into the room, cowering back in horror from the glass. Some had ducked under their desks.

'Boys,' said Harrow. 'I told you to get BACK.'

As the Cleve spoke the final word his fingers twisted sharply.

Vershan and Tarawen flew backwards across the room. Darion ducked as his friends soared over his head. Their arms windmilled wildly in the air and their legs kicked out frantically to stay upright. A moment later Harrow clenched his fist and both landed safely on their feet near to their desks.

Everyone's mouths were now wide open. The students didn't know where to look; at the fearsome brannoch, who even now was crouching down ready to leap at the cracked glass; at Vershan and Tarawen swaying unsteadily after their flight; or at their teacher, who suddenly seemed much more interesting than he ever had before.

Cleve Harrow pulled his hand from his pocket. He continued to move swiftly towards the window. Darion saw a small vial of liquid in his fingers.

'Everyone down,' he said. This time no one disobeyed. They all ducked behind their desks and chairs immediately.

Darion peered from behind his desk and saw Harrow fling his arm wide. The liquid in the bottle flew out towards the window just as the brannoch launched itself once more. 'It must get through this time,' Darion thought. 'We're done for.'

But the liquid from the Cleve's bottle hit the glass a fraction of a second before their attacker did. There was a loud hiss, like steam escaping form a giant kettle, and the window seemed to seal itself again. The brannoch hit it with all its force. There was another terrifying thud. Everyone flinched backwards, many of them screamed again, but the window held.

When it realised that it could not get at its prey, the brannoch became even more enraged. It slavered hungrily and snapped at the glass with its teeth. Its club hands beat against the glass time and again, making it rattle in the frame, but still it could not break through the seal which Harrow had thrown against it.

Darion heard a familiar sound. The long wailing cry of a hunting horn. *'It must be Matthien and the others,'* he thought.

Sure enough the brannoch stopped looking in at them. It turned its head and stared down into the courtyard. The double oak gates at the far side burst open. The students craned their necks from their hiding places to see Matthien, Jorian and Bargoth gallop through. Darion saw Zarak racing ahead. His master was blowing hard on the hunting horn. Behind him, Jorian dropped his own reins and reached behind him. He brought out a long bow, swiftly notching an arrow to it as he rode.

There was a cheer from Vershan and a couple of the others as they watched this new excitement, but Darion could only stand and stare in silence.

Jorian released his first arrow towards the brannoch. It flew wide of its target and clattered against the window. Even Vershan jumped back. Jorian had already prepared another arrow, and let it fly. It was immediately followed by one from Matthien's bow.

The brannoch howled in anger, turned briefly to give one final snap at the classroom window, then leapt away. As it did, two glistening wings unfolded from the muscles of its back and it lurched into the air.

Harrow watched, as fascinated as the rest of them, as the beast rose up from the centre of the courtyard. With another flap it reached the height of the rooftops.

'Well,' Darion heard Harrow murmur, 'I've never seen one do that bef...'

His words were cut off by the call of a different horn.

Darion snapped his attention back down to the courtyard. Alianna was now riding in through the gates. She looked up at the horrific creature flying above her. Darion's heart lurched again as he thought of the sudden danger she was in. Without looking away from her target for a moment, Alianna rose up in her stirrups and pointed her finger straight at the escaping brannoch. He saw her lips move, but couldn't tell what she was saying, or think who she might be talking to. A second later there was a bright flash of incandescent light and a dull thumping explosion. The sound reminded Darion of the market cannon being fired on the first day of the Beltheron Festa.

'Now that's the way to do it,' Vershan yelled delightedly. Darion followed his friend's gaze back up to the brannoch. It had burst into a ball of flame in the air.

Matthien and the other riders spurred their horses away from the middle of the courtyard. They were just in time to shelter under the wide eaves as the burning beast came crashing down.

All of the students cheered loudly. Now there was nothing that the Cleve could say to make them stay in their seats. They all ran to the miraculously mended window and gazed out at their new heroes.

'Bet you didn't see that coming,' Vershan said to Korellia as she pushed in next to him to get a good view.

Darion was the only one who stayed at his desk. He stared hard at the Cleve. His tutor slumped back behind his desk. He was nursing the hand that he had used to fling Vershan and Tarawen across the room. Darion watched him gently massage the fingers with his other hand. The Cleve looked exhausted. He glanced up and saw the boy watching him. 'Sir, are you alright, sir?'

Harrow nodded.

'I just need a moment.'

The others now started to turn back from the window. The fire was still blazing outside, but they had their own questions for the Cleve.

'Sir, that was amazing.'

'How did you do that?'

'Are you a mage, sir?'

'Do it again!'

'Make me fly, like you did with Vershan and Tarawen, sir!'

He waved them to silence and got to his feet.

'Everyone in your seats,' he said. 'Now please, Master Vershan, Master Tarawen. Come away from that window at once or I will be obliged to *hurl* you again.'

There was laughter, and a few cheers from the others in the room.

'Hurl *us* sir! They've already had a go.'

'Yes sir, it's not fair. Give us a turn too!'

There was more laughter. The Cleve silenced it again. Now all that could be heard was the sound of a few urgent, whispered questions as they started to move back to their seats;

'But how did he do it?'

'Who is he?'

'Just think! Our teacher, a mage!'

'That will do,' Harrow continued, when everyone had finally taken their places. 'Listen to me carefully. There are a few things I need to tell you.'

Harrow's Secrets

'Let us begin with what you know,' Harrow said. 'You are all here to study the art of essence hunting. After your primus education all of you in this room have chosen this type of additional or *continuum* course. All of you made the choice personally, as something which you felt you had a fondness for, a subject that excited you.

'Essence hunting is an art form, but it also involves science. It is, I believe, one of the finest courses of study, for it allows us to achieve our full potential as individuals. It can, if taken seriously and studied hard, allow us to learn more about who we really are, and it gives us tools to make the most of ourselves.'

He paused and looked around. They knew this already. It had been spelled out for them last year when they made their course choices at 11 years old. But every pair of eyes remained on his, riveted. They knew he had much more to tell them. Everyone waited for an explanation about the sudden revelation of Cleve Harrow's surprising skills.

'There is, however, another side to essence hunting,' Harrow continued. 'It forms part of a much larger study, a kind of magic I suppose, that only a few of you will ever begin to learn fully. Over the years I have become an *ament*, one who is adept and skilful at using the essences to their full extent. Darion rolled the strange word around in his mouth: *'ament'*. He had never heard it before.

Hands started to shoot up from every part of the class. They all had questions. Harrow waved them down and continued.

'The things that you have just witnessed me perform have all been mastered by years of study. Making that cracked window secure; giving our young colleagues here a flying lesson,' he gestured towards Vershan and Tarawen. Their faces went bright red while everyone else in the room sniggered.

Harrow waved them to silence again. 'But these are all skills that have to be carefully practised and controlled. Otherwise they can cause no end of damage and danger.'

'Are you a mage sir?' Vershan asked. It was what many of his classmates had been thinking. The room was thick with silence as they waited to hear the Cleve's answer.

Harrow looked at him and smiled. 'I prefer the term *ament*, my boy. But if mage is the word you wish to use, then yes, I am a mage.'

An immediate burble and hum of gossip thrummed throughout the room. Harrow waited for the hubbub to die down again.

'After seeing such things this morning, some of you will be excited and want to begin learning such things yourselves...'

'Absolutely sir!' said Bedellya, her hand straight up in the air with enthusiasm. 'I want to be an ament like you sir!'

'...but I must caution you with patience,' the Cleve continued. 'Patience and conscience about how you use such skills.

'There are of course, others who have no wish to master such things. Some of you may feel threatened by power such as this; that you would not feel comfortable pursuing it.'

Harrow paused and looked around at the class. He was right. Some of them still looked terrified by what they had seen him do. Darion himself looked away, unable to meet the Cleve's eyes.

'No one must feel as if they have failed, or are in any way inferior, just because they do not wish to continue their studies in this way. Not everyone is the same. This level of study is not for everyone.'

Harrow paused again. He seemed uncertain whether to continue or not. When he did speak again it was in a voice so hushed that Darion had to strain to hear the words.

'I spoke of conscience a moment ago,' he said. 'There are those who wish to use essencing for other ends.' He glanced around the corners of the room, as if he thought someone might be lurking there, listening. 'Some are already seeking ways of using what we teach for darker, more dangerous reasons. Beware of them, and of following a similar path yourselves.'

No one else spoke. There was such a sadness, and a fear in Cleve Harrow's face that it struck them all into silence. They all understood the seriousness of what he said.

He shook his head quickly as if to shake away his dark thoughts.

'Well, after the excitements of the morning we will finish early,' he said. 'I declare the lessons over for today. And as we did not proceed with the class as normal, I have no further homework to give to you this evening.'

Everyone grinned and looked at each other. There were a few murmured 'Phews" from a number of students. Only Bedellya looked disappointed. Darion gave a greater sigh of relief than anyone else. At least the secret of his broken jar was safe for a little longer.

As he and Vershan walked back across the courtyard Matthien came running up to them.

'You were awesome,' Vershan said. His eyes were wide with admiration. The young lord nodded briefly at him then turned to Darion.

'Darion, may I have a word?'

He drew him to one side.

'My friend, there's a ball being held in the Variegatt Great Hall this evening. I would enjoy it very much if you could join me there.'

Darion didn't know what to say.

'Me, sir?'

'None of that 'sir' business. Matthien, or Matt, is fine. Now would you like to come along?'

Darion glanced at Vershan who was eavesdropping on the conversation. His friend's eyes were as wide as a draccen's spreading wings.

'I...I'm not sure if I...'

'Go on,' whispered Vershan, who had edged nearer. 'You can't give up a chance like this.'

'But...'

Then Darion thought about Alianna. She was sure to be there. He would love to see her again. And he wanted to congratulate her on defeating the brannoch.

'All right, thank you,' he said to Matthien. 'I'd love to come.'

But how would he fit in at such a party? And what would he say to all of those wealthy people in the Variegatt?

Banquet in the Variegatt

Before he could even think of joining his new friends at a fancy banquet, he knew that he would have to get past his mother's questions. She was bound to disapprove. He could almost hear her using one of her favourite phrases: *'you're climbing above yourself my boy; you'll fall out of your own fancies if you're not careful.'*

But this wasn't him being fanciful, not this time. He had an invitation to join a great party. He had made new friends. And he couldn't stop thinking about the fact that Alianna would be there.

He raced faster than usual around the street corner. The sooner he got the conversation with his mother over and done with, the sooner he would be on his way. Beskar the dog barked his usual gruff warning from next door, but Darion hardly heard him. He raced into the kitchen area.

'Why the hurry?' His mother was standing by the stove, steam curling from an old rusted pan in her gloved hands. She placed it impatiently on top of the ancient table, slipped the gloves from her fingers and reached for a wooden spoon.

'Is it alright if I go out this evening?' he asked. He hoped his voice did not sound too desperate. He wouldn't get his way if she thought he was whining. His mother hated whiners, and never lost a chance to tell him so.

'Again?' she said.

This was unfair. He deserved a break from the studying. He worked hard at it all day. She always made it sound as though he were out all of the time. In fact, he thought bitterly, he stayed at home almost every night during the week. Vershan and most of the others in his class spent far more time at each others' houses or roaming up and down the Tenementerra streets than he was ever allowed. Of course he didn't dare voice any of this to his mother.

'Your studies can't be as interesting as you make out if you don't want to spend time on them in the evening,' his mother continued.

He stayed silent, his head sunk low on his chest.

'And you can lift your chin up too young man,' she went on. 'Don't throw any sulks onto me. It's as bad as whining – worse even.'

He sighed under his breath and hoped she didn't hear. Sighing was probably as bad as whining and sulking.

'Ok,' he said. He was just resigning himself to the fact he was not going to be allowed out, when he heard himself speak again. 'But it *is* to study,' he said. The words were out of his mouth before he had thought about them properly. He hated lying to his mother. But the lie was there now. He couldn't take it back.

'To study?'

He nodded. 'We have a project to finish,' he blurted. 'Vershan and me, we…'

'Vershan and I,' his mother corrected.

'Vershan and I. The Cleve has set us an experiment and we both need to do it together. To… to…compare notes and results.'

She turned away from him and sat at the table. It seemed she had already lost interest. 'Very well, if it is for the Cleve,' she said. 'But don't be late back.'

*   *   *   *

Darion always thought that the Variegatt looked like an immense iced cake, piled up in layers. High smooth walls rose up in a wide arc at the western end of the city. They were not the dull, dry clay colour of the Tementerra, but decorated in pastel shades that reminded him of icing. A pair of golden gates opened up from these smooth walls onto a broad road beyond. He had peered through those gates once, when he had been exploring the city with Vershan. The road was patterned with a mosaic of brightly coloured stones and pebbles. *'Like a picture you can walk on,'* he thought. He had always imagined that one day he would walk through these gates and onto those streets himself. And now it was about to happen.

The golden gates were wide enough for four horses to pass through side by side. As he approached them he looked up at the beautiful carvings and statues of bronze, gold and jewels that surrounded them. He gulped hard. Again he wondered about how on earth he was ever going to be able to find his way around. Who could he talk to when he was on the other side?

He needn't have worried. Matt was already there, waiting to greet him as he walked up the main street into the shadow of the gates. The young lord was wearing a pedjiaar costume. The tunic fitted him tightly and was beautifully stitched with red, grey and silver stripes. A cloak curled up from around his shoulders and over his face like a mask. It covered the top part of his head and looked just like the face of one of the big cats, complete with whiskers and open jaws with rows of jagged teeth.

His new friend grinned excitedly.

'You're here,' he said. 'I'm really glad you could make it. Here, take these. I didn't know whether you would know to bring your own costume. This is an old one of mine.' He handed Darion a bright cloak and a half-mask with a long handle. Eye holes had been cut out of an expensive looking piece of decorated leather. It had been painted with the colours of a peacock's wings. Real feathers sprouted from the eyebrows. Darion thought it was one of the most beautiful things he had ever seen. He held it up to his face and crowed at Matthien, imitating the cries of the exotic birds he had seen in the city parks.

'That's the way,' his friend grinned at him. 'Now throw that cloak over your shoulders.'

Darion did as he was told. The material fluttered around him like wings. It seemed to have a life of its own. He grinned at his new friend again.

'Thanks, I don't know what to say.'

'No need, no need. Just get into the spirit of it. These masked balls are usually a screech.'

This strange phrase confused Darion for a moment, until he realised that 'a screech' must mean 'great fun'.

They made their way through the lantern-lit streets of the Variegatt. He gazed around him, trying to take in every detail he could. He had promised to make a full report of the evening to Vershan. He wanted to make sure that he didn't miss a thing.

High overhead he heard a thin ragged squawk. In the same instant a series of shadows threw the street into darkness. He looked up to see the shape of three huge draccen flying among the rooftops. They were heading for the palace. He could just make out the billowing green capes of their riders. They were steering the winged beasts with reins and whips.

'Representatives from the city of Maraglar,' Matthien explained. 'Merchants and traders. Lord Argolin will use every opportunity tonight to make business deals. It's partly for the good of the Guild, but mainly to increase his own fortune. That's the only reason they're invited.'

Darion knew about the Guild. It pretty much owned the city and most of its businesses. Many of the wealthy people from the Variegatt belonged to it.

He watched the flight of the draccen until they disappeared over the rooftops at the end of the street. Then he heard their cries again. They sounded lower down this time. '*They must be coming in to land,*' he thought to himself.

'Come on,' Matthien said, 'We're nearly there. Let's go and see them up close.'

They hurried down the street. Two steps at a time they climbed the staircase that led up to the palace. Moments later they were standing in a huge courtyard at the top. The palace rose in front of them. The three draccen had already landed. They were stamping their clawed feet on the cobbles. Their elegant riders were dismounting and handing the reins to servants on the lower steps. Many of them looked extremely nervous at being so close to the winged beasts.

Darion held back for a moment.

'It's quite alright. They're harmless,' Matthien told him. 'Unless you surprise or anger one of them. Then watch out for their breath!'

As if to prove what he said, one of the draccen let out a rasping cry at one of the servants holding its reins and a flicker of flame spat towards him. The young man cried out and staggered backwards. He dropped the reins and tripped over a step, landing heavily at the feet of one of the Maraglar merchants. The man spat angrily, flicking his green robes away from the unfortunate servant as if he were a patch of mud that threatened to splash his finery.

As they approached, Darion noticed that the men from Maraglar were the only ones not wearing fancy dress.

Everyone else had elaborate costumes like Matthien. Many were dressed as animals, but he also saw pirates, storybook wizards and jesters.

He knew that each one of those costumes must have cost more than he or his mother had ever spent on clothes in their whole lives.

Matt looked at him. It seemed he was reading Darion's mind.

'It's different here,' he said. 'You can't judge it in the same way as other places in the city.'

Darion nodded. 'Ok.' He still couldn't help an uncomfortable feeling of jealousy though. And he couldn't help thinking for a moment about why the Variegatt couldn't be judged on its behaviour just because it was wealthy. He wondered what would happen to all of those fine costumes when this evening was over. He looked down again at the 'old' costume Matthien had leant him. The colours were still fresh and bright, the fabric soft. It couldn't have been worn more than once or twice, he thought.

Up they went, past the snorting, steaming draccen, up past the guards who nodded at Matthien, up past the carved doors and into the heart of the palace. Here was yet another staircase, leading even higher into the vast building, up to the great hall itself where the ball was being held.

This staircase glowed with light. There were glistening chandeliers high up on the ceiling that had more candles in them than Darion imagined were used in his part of the city in a whole year. But even more lanterns had been hung along the sides of the steps. They flickered and gleamed as Darion made his way to the doors at the top. It made everything as bright as a summer noontime. He looked at the gentlemen and elegant Variegatt women moving smoothly between each other, laughing and talking in rich, deep tones. How could he ever get through meeting such people without making a fool of himself? Already he could feel his face growing hot.

Darion swallowed hard. He paused on the stairs. Part of him wanted to turn around and run back home again.

'Don't worry,' Matt said. 'You'll find that we're a friendly lot, in spite of the stories you might have heard in the Tenementerra.'

Darion hoped so, even though the memory of Jorian leapt to his mind. He hadn't proved to be very friendly yesterday, he thought. But no matter how nervous he felt, Darion knew that the party would be worth it. Vershan would never believe any of this. Darion was already looking forward to telling him all about it tomorrow.

Two guards stood at the top of the stairs, at either side of the wide brass doors.

Matt led him through the doors. Darion's mouth gaped open. There were delicate carvings in the brass of the doorframe. They showed images of hunters on horseback, spears flashing, pedjiaar and other big cats cowering in terror. He gulped as he thought about his experiences of the day before. They weren't just scaring away predators in these carvings, they were killing them. The artist must have been very skilful, for the excitement and cruelty in the hunters' eyes was plain to see.

Matthien was gesturing for him to move on. He had to drag his eyes away from the horror of the carvings.

They walked through and into the great hall.

Here, a thick scent of honey and roses almost made him dizzy. Looking to his right he saw a boy of about nine years old. His clothes looked thin and scratchy. The boy slowly turned the handle of a large wooden construction. It had a vast leather balloon at the back. As the boy cranked the handle two brass arms squeezed the balloon. Darion felt it blow a gust of air towards him and another strong waft of flowery perfume filled his nostrils. '*Clever,*' 'Darion thought. He stood for a moment, admiring the machine. '*But I wonder how long that boy has to stand there turning the handle? All night I suppose.*'

'Fine building isn't it?' Matthien said.

Darion just nodded. He was so amazed by the splendour he was seeing that he couldn't think of any reply.

'These rooms go back for some way, right to the edge of the city,' his new friend continued. 'My house is the building next door. Running underneath here are my father's wine cellars. They used to be the dungeons.'

At last, Darion found his voice. 'They must go for miles,' he said.

'Well, maybe not miles, but certainly a long, long way into the hillsides,' Matthien replied. 'My ancestors had dozens and dozens of dungeons down there. Come on.'

Further down the crowded hall Alianna was waving at him. He grinned as he saw her. She came towards him and grabbed his hand. Her perfume mingled with the scent coming from the machine. He recognised the same mix of honeysuckle and spices from the day before.

'You made it! I'm so glad that Matt convinced you to come. It's wonderful to see you.'

Alianna was dressed as some kind of bird of paradise. Long multi-coloured feathers flowed down from her shoulders like silken wings, and she wore a full length evening gown that rippled like water and made Darion think of the fountains and pools in the city parks. She led him further into the hall. Straightaway Alianna was relaxed and talkative but he found it hard to say much in reply. He only managed to blurt out a mangled, 'Thanks, good to see you too,' when she first greeted him. This wasn't like chatting with Vershan, or talking to anyone else in the Tenementerra. He knew he couldn't tease this young woman in the same way that he joked with the other girls in his class. When he did that, it made him feel clever in front of the other boys. It made people laugh. He knew that Alianna would just find his sense of humour boring, and a bit stupid.

'Oh!' she noticed. 'You don't have a pin.'

'A what?'

'A pin, you know, here,' Alianna pointed at a bright button on her own collar. 'Everyone is wearing them.'

He looked around and sure enough, everyone else had a small metal brooch like hers fastened to their costumes. He suddenly realised he had seen Matt wearing one too. 'They're for a game at the end of the night,' she said. 'Here, take mine, I can get another later.' She reached up and unclipped the colourful brooch from the strap of her costume. She began to fasten it to the lapel of his cloak, near his throat. He moved his head back nervously.

The pin pricked his neck.

'Ouch!'

'Sorry, you should keep still.'

He reached up to feel his throat. His finger came away with a smear of blood on it.

'Here, let me,' Alianna said. She dabbed at the wound with a handkerchief. 'There, all better.' The handkerchief disappeared into her pocket and she whisked him away through the crowds. She led him to a wooden sideboard which ran along the full length of one of the walls. Arranged on top were over one hundred small vials. Coloured liquid swirled around inside each one of these little bottles, and there were patterns painted on the outside in similar colours.

'The colours and the design on your pin matches one of these vials,' Alianna explained. 'In the game you have to take just a small drop on the end of one of these.' There was a bunch of small straws with bubbles at one end sticking up out of a large glass jar on the sideboard, like tiny arrows in a quiver. She picked one up and dipped the straw into the nearest vial. Alianna carefully squeezed the bubble between her fingers. As she released her fingers again a few drops of the liquid were drawn up into the straw. 'Not too much,' she warned him, 'It's just to give you the sense of being another creature. It helps you to act out your charade, so that everyone else can try to guess what you are.'

'Is that what the game is?' he asked. 'Just acting out charades?' They had done this in his first-days class at school, when he had been little.

She laughed. 'Not like any game you've played before! It's not just like acting out a phrase or an action for someone else to guess. This is imagining you're something else entirely. At the Festa last year my pin was jet black. There was a feather decorating it. I was meant to be a raven in the game, so I searched for a black vial and took some. It made it easier to act it out for everyone and I even managed to float up into the air for a few moments when I flapped my arms. It's fun pretending to be something else don't you think?'

'And the liquid does that? Helps you to fly?' He was now staring hard at the small bottles, fascinated. He knew that really this was just another kind of essencing, but this was much more exciting than the Cleve had ever made it sound in his classes.

'I don't suppose it was anything like proper flying,' Alianna said. 'But it felt amazing to float – even though it was only for a couple of seconds.' Her eyes were brighter than ever as she described it. 'It's not just floating either. The different colours all help you do different things.'

'They're like our essences that we use in class,' he said, finally finding his voice. 'Of course, what we're working on in our studies is much more serious.' He hoped that he wasn't sounding too self-important.

'A bit like that yes. But these have been changed quite a bit by the game-mages I would think.'

Darion wondered if what the game-mages had done made the essences dangerous. Harrow was always warning them not to mess around with the potions.

'Some give you an incredible sense of smell like a dog, or the strength and speed of a horse,' she continued. 'Last year, I remember Matthien's pin was a reddish brown. Brown with little flecks of white. His vial made him cunning like a silkefox. It was like that red one over there.' She pointed to another of the vials, filled with a beautiful russet liquid that shone like a late sunset. 'It lets you outwit anyone else. Like a silkefox can outrun and out-think nearly every hunter.' She giggled as she remembered. 'We played a game of hide-seek afterwards and we couldn't find Matt for the rest of the night.'

Alianna picked up a bottle filled with a bright liquid. Darion noticed that it matched the colours of the pin she had given him.

'Do you...do you want me to take it now?' he asked her. His knees felt funny all of a sudden.

'Not yet,' she replied. 'The game won't start until the feasting is over and everyone has had a chance to dance at least twice.'

Darion felt a surge of relief. There was something strange, something he didn't trust about the little bottles of liquid.

'We won't get around to the games until much later,' Alianna continued. 'Come on I'm hungry.'

They started to move back towards the food tables. As they made their way across the room he saw that Matthien had moved off to greet more people. He was now in the middle of a group of young lords. They were all laughing loudly. Darion's heart hammered in his chest at their noise and confidence.

Even with Alianna beside him he still felt shy and nervous. What would these people expect of him? And what would they think of his shabby clothes? The cloak that Matthien had given him as a costume was good quality of course. Even so it only just about covered his baggy shirt and scuffed trousers; he had managed to fix his boot for now, but it was only a matter of time before the sole came unstuck again. He knew that he looked nothing like the finery and splendour all around him.

He needn't have worried. In another moment, they had reached the group of boys and Alianna was introducing him. Matt immediately slapped Darion on the shoulder before grasping his hand tightly in both his own, telling the others all about how they had met. His eyes glittered with pleasure.

Whatever Darion had ever thought about the people of the Variegatt before, it certainly didn't match his experience of the young folk at the party that night. His mother had told him that they would be snobbish and stand-offish; that they would feel embarrassed to be seen talking to him and would make an excuse to leave him as soon as possible. Nothing could have been further from the truth. They chatted away and seemed to be genuinely interested in his experiences as a student with the Cleve, and about his home and life in the Tenementerra streets.

Matthien in particular asked him a lot of questions about his studies.

'Essencing has an important part to play in the city you know,' said Halperth, a boy just a little older than Matthien. 'Lord Argolin says that if the Guild can control the way the mages create…'

'Enough Halperth,' Matthien cut in. 'Darry's having a night off from his studies, aren't you Darry?'

Halperth looked uncomfortable for a moment, and

Darion wondered what it was he had been about to say. It seemed as if Matthien was cross with him, for when he looked back at him, Matt was staring sternly at Halperth.

Matt saw Darion watching him. The expression on his face changed and he grinned. 'It is a party after all,' he said. 'You don't want to hear about the boring old history of the mages and the Guild do you Darry?'

'Well, I don't really kn…' Darion found it hard to answer him. 'What *do* the members of the Guild have to do with essencing anyw…'

'Exactly,' Matt interrupted. 'Probably nothing at all. And probably not as exciting as the experiments that you are all doing in your class, eh Darry?'

He slapped him on the back again, almost knocking Darion off his feet.

'If you don't mind, Darry, I'll join you in your class again tomorrow.'

Before he had chance to reply, Darion heard another familiar voice over his shoulder.

'Well well, I see that Matthien is still slumming it with his new gutterboy friend.'

He turned and saw Jorian standing behind him. Darion realised that so far he had only ever seen Jorian on horseback. Now he stood so close he was surprised at how tall the young man was. He towered over Darion. His shoulders and chest were as high as the top of Darion's head and his arms were broad and powerful looking. Darion felt his stomach turn over in dread.

Jorian was dressed as a draccen.

His mask had a long, narrow snout opening into wide nostrils. A pair of leathery wings curled from his shoulders like a cape. They draped down to the floor, where they made a rasping snake's hiss against the tiles as Jorian moved.

'Well, gutterboy, do you have nothing to say?' Jorian spat.

'Leave him alone Jorian, he's done nothing to you,' said Matt.

Jorian sneered in reply. 'Well just make sure it stays that way.'

He turned away. Seeing Alianna standing nearby, he took hold of her arm. 'Come on Ali,' he said. 'I want to introduce you to some *real* friends of mine.'

Darion's stomach tightened at the thought that Alianna was not going to stay with them. He *wanted* to say something, but his tongue felt as if it was stuck to the roof of his mouth. Alianna just about managed to smile a quick apology at him before Jorian had steered her off through the crowds.

'I'm sorry about him,' Matt said. 'Jorian comes from a fine family. His father is the High Lord.'

'Jorian's father is Lord Argolin?'

'That's right, he's one of the wealthiest people in the Variegatt. He runs teams of Guild merchants and traders all the way to Maraglar City, but I'm afraid that sometimes his son can forget his manners. I apologise on his behalf.'

Darion shrugged. 'It's ok. Look, he's not happy about me being here. Maybe I should go?'

'Not a bit, not a bit. You haven't even eaten yet. And you have a pin now, I see. That's good, that's good. It means you can join the game later.'

'Alianna gave me the pin.' Darion realised he enjoyed saying her name.

'Did she? Good, good.'

'And Alianna started to tell me, about the game I mean, but I'm still not sure I understand the rules?'

Matthien appeared not to hear him. He looked across at the food tables.

'I'm starving. Let's introduce ourselves to the buffet. I can tell you all about it while we eat.'

The Draccen's Threat

Darion began moving around the outside of the hall. They had finished eating. The food had left him with a warm glow and he felt contented and happy. If only he could see Alianna again and chat to her a bit more.

He craned his neck to see over the heads of the adults dancing in front of him, trying to get a glimpse of her, or of Matt.

A couple of the rich merchants he had seen arriving on their draccen earlier were talking nearby.

'Arteris is still in charge,' said the first.

'Not for much longer if the Maraglar merchants' gossip about Argolin is anything to go by.'

The words drew Darion's attention to their conversation. It was the second time that night that he had heard Argolin and Maraglar merchants mentioned.

'Believe me,' the second man continued. 'Lord Argolin and Gretton Tur will soon have their way. The word is they're getting closer to success all the time. Argolin will be able to ask for whatever he wants. And Maraglar won't have a choice but to agree to his terms. They won't dare; Argolin and Tur are near to getting the midst...'

Then, Darion felt a hand on his arm. It pulled him back so sharply that he lost his balance and fell against a table. He put out his hand to steady himself and it landed in a plate of half eaten chicken and sauce. A couple of glasses toppled over and smashed. The noise made a few of the people nearby turn to look.

'Idiot boy, now look what you have done,' said a familiar voice.

It was Jorian, of course. His eyes glittered through the scaly draccen mask. He tightened his grip on Darion's arm as he spat out the words. Darion looked around desperately for Matt, but he was nowhere to be seen. The adults nearby had turned away again almost immediately, unconcerned about what they thought was just a clumsy younger boy being reprimanded by one of the lords. Jorian grabbed Darion by the collar and hauled him into a corner of the room. He glanced quickly around the room then pushed Darion behind the heavy curtains. Jorian followed him quickly and pulled the drapes closed behind them.

Darion found himself standing next to the older boy on a small balcony. It was open to the night air and he felt a prickle of gooselumps as the cold breeze hit their faces. Darion realised that out here they couldn't be seen by anyone else in the hall. The way the older boy had looked around a moment ago to make sure no one was watching made Darion's legs feel as if they had turned to water. At that moment the orchestra in the main hall began playing again. It would drown out any noise they made. There was no way anyone would hear them now either. His stomach made a sickening slide of fear.

Jorian pulled his draccen mask up onto the top of his head and Darion could see the gleam of evil excitement in his eyes.

'What makes you think that a dreg of urchin scum like you belongs here?' he spat. His chin was raised up as he gazed down in contempt at Darion. It was meant to be menacing. It would have worked, but it meant that Darion was looking right up Jorian's nose. He could see that in spite of all the Variegatt boy's fine costume and oiled hair, he had forgotten to use a handkerchief before coming to the ball. His nostrils were clogged with snot.

In spite of his fear at the beating he knew must be coming, Darion found it hard to disguise a grin.

'Are you laughing at me, you shred?'

Darion shook his head firmly. 'No Jorian, I mean, sir, not at all, sir.' As he spoke, he carried on looking at the way Jorian's nostrils flared with anger. A small dribble of mucus began running out of his attacker's nose towards his top lip. Darion's nervous fear made a giggle rise up again. Laughing was the last thing he felt like doing, the last thing that he *should* do in front of this powerful bully, but it was hard to stop it. He coughed loudly.

'Are you *still* laughing, you little villain?'

'No sir.'

'Because I'll strike it off your face with my fist if you are.'

'No, really, sir.'

Perhaps it was the cold wind on the balcony that was making his nose run so much, Darion thought. The drip had now reached Jorian's mouth. It drooped over his top lip and hung there over his snarling teeth. Darion's smile widened even more. He tried to stamp down on it, forcing his mouth into a serious line.

'Would you *like* me to strike you, you dirty shred?'

'No, sir, I don't mean to offend you sir.'

Jorian bent down closer to Darion until his face was only a few centimetres away. The snot dangled and wobbled around Jorian's lips. He breathed in and the line of mucous threatened to disappear into his mouth.

Darion clenched his teeth together, to force back the fearful laugh that still threatened to burst out of him

'Well. You'd. Better. Not.' Jorian stabbed his finger into Darion's chest with each word.

Darion shook his head. 'No sir. I won't sir.'

Jorian straightened up again. Darion breathed a sigh of relief. Perhaps he had got away with it.

Then Jorian gave a great, loud sniff. The dribble of slimy snot was sucked back up into his cavernous nose as he turned away. It disappeared like a worm down a bird's throat.

That was it. With a loud *'Pah!'* the laughter burst out of Darion like an exploding cannon.

Jorian had opened the curtains back into the hall. They could now be seen by the adults at the party inside. At that moment, the orchestra had reached a quieter part of their music.

Darion's laugh was so loud that it stopped everyone's conversation. All of the lords and fine women nearby turned to look.

Jorian froze. He had only taken a couple of steps. He was still turned away from Darion; one hand still gripped the drapes of the curtain. Darion felt all of his fear returning as he saw his enemy's shoulders rise slightly. The movement made the draccen wings on the bully's costume flutter realistically. Darion's hysterical laughter faded immediately in his throat and in the sudden silence he could hear his own heart thudding rapidly. The fingers of Jorian's left hand tightened on the curtain. His other hand closed firmly into a fist.

'Did. You. Just. *Laugh?*'

Darion was fixed to the spot in terror. He couldn't speak; couldn't move. He looked at Jorian's clenched fist. He imagined the damage those huge hands were about to do to him. Darion flinched away and instinctively clenched his stomach muscles, getting ready for the first blow.

'Answer me, you toad. DID – YOU – JUST - LAUGH?'

Jorian spun around. Before Darion could even move, the larger boy's hand was around his windpipe. He felt his throat being squeezed. Darion choked, struggling to breathe. He was aware of the curtain closing, cutting off his escape. The loud swirl of music started up again.

From the corner of his eye, he could see Jorian's other hand still bunched into a fist. It came in fast towards his stomach. He twisted around to try to avoid the punch. The pain in his throat increased, but at least it softened the blow to his body. In his anger Jorian had mis-timed his attack and his fist landed softly, glancing off Darion's side. The older boy winced as he grazed his knuckles on the wall behind him.

'Don't move this time,' Jorian told him. 'It'll only make it worse for you.'

Tears stung his eyes as Darion waited for the second blow. The fingers dug even more cruelly into his throat. Darion still couldn't breathe. He felt dizzy. His vision started to blur as he fought for air. He knew that he was going to pass out.

Then the curtains swished open. A huge shadow fell across them both.

'What in the seer's bloody fangs is going on?'

The voice was angry and full of authority. Jorian stopped instantly and Darion felt a surge of relief as the pressure on his neck was released. Jorian let go of him and Darion slid back against the wall. He made a soft choking sound as he gulped down air.

A tall figure stood in the opening of the curtains. Darion's eyes still watered. Bright flashes exploded in his vision as he struggled to look at the man. He couldn't make out much detail of the face. He didn't need to; it was clear that the man was furious.

'This is one of the most important nights in our calendar,' he said. 'It is to be expected that *you* Jorian, the son of the High Lord of the Guild, act with a level of decorum and politeness which is beyond reproach. It does *not* mean that you should carry on like a grubby wretch who picks fights with those beneath him.'

Jorian stood stiffly. Darion could see his chest heave in and out, and the muscles of his jaw were now clenched as tightly as his fists had been moments earlier.

Things dropped into place in Darion's head. This man was obviously Jorian's father, Lord Argolin himself, the High Lord of the Guild of Beltheron. This was one of the most powerful and important men in the city.

As he stepped closer to them, a shaft of light from the ballroom lit up the man's face. Cruel and angry, a long scar wound from his left eyebrow, down the side of his nose and ended in a puckered red slash across his cheek.

'But Father,' Jorian started to reply. He didn't get to say anything else. Another figure stepped forwards. It was Bargoth, one of the other hunters that Darion had met in the forest. He placed his hand firmly on Jorian's shoulder.

'Steady lad,' Bargoth said.

Jorian tried to pull away in embarrassment, but Bargoth's grip was too strong. Tears of frustration sprang up in Jorian's eyes. His mouth had clenched so tightly to stop his tears that Darion thought he might crack his own teeth.

Argolin looked down at Darion with contempt. He felt like a slug, or something horrible on the sole of the High Lord's shoe.

'I haven't seen you before,' Argolin said to him. 'And I certainly don't expect to see you again.' He leaned in closer, his eyes flickering with fury. 'The seers only know how you got in here, but if you're *still* here in thirty seconds you'll be leaving by flying over this balcony on the end of my boot.'

Lord Argolin turned away, all his thoughts of Darion immediately disappearing.

'Now, Jorian,' his father continued in a steadier voice. 'The Halicon family have been expecting to meet you all evening. Belius Halicon is an important business connection of mine. He made a special journey from Maraglar to be here tonight and I expect you to present yourself to him immediately. Offer him and his family whatever drinks or tidbits they require.'

'Yes Father.'

'Make me proud, Jorian.'

'Yes Father.'

'No more messing around with the Tenementerra scum.'

Darion could see the shame in Jorian's eyes. He knew the humiliation that he must be feeling. To be told off by his father like that in front of a boy from the Tenementerra would burn at the young lord's pride. The thought didn't give Darion any satisfaction though. If Jorian had been his enemy before, then he was even more so now. Filled with more resentment for Darion, and much, *much* more dangerous. Argolin started to move off into the crowds of dancing couples.

'And Jorian,' he called behind him.

'Yes Father?'

'Wipe your nose. You look like a street urchin.'

Lord Argolin marched down the hall with his cloak billowing out behind him like a mainsail on one of his trading ships. Everyone moved back to give him a clear passage through the centre of the room.

Jorian spun around to face Darion once more. Pulling Bargoth's hand from his shoulder he descended on his prey. He pushed his face into Darion's again until he could feel the young lord's hot breath on his face.

Jorian's eyes were wet and glistened with rage. He was breathing heavily. He stabbed his finger into Darion's chest.

'This isn't over,' he whispered. 'I'll be watching and waiting. I'll get my chance. Think of that. You'll wish we'd never found you in those damned bushes.' Then he spun away and walked briskly down the hall after his father.

Moments later, Matthien hurried up to him.

'What is wrong with Jorian and his father?' he said. 'I've never seen Argolin so angry.'

'I'm sorry Matt,' Darion began. 'It wasn't my fault, but Jorian started to argue with me and...'

'Jorian,' Matthien said. 'I might have guessed it.' His eyes narrowed.

'But it wasn't my fault, Matt, I was just...'

'You must listen to me my friend,' Matt interrupted. 'Jorian is not someone you want to cross. It would be most foolish to make an enemy of him. Steer clear of Argolin and all of his family.'

Darion thought this advice was a bit too late.

'After Lord Arteris himself, Argolin is the most powerful man in the city.' Matt continued. 'But as you have already found out he is hot-headed and easy to anger.' He paused and grinned. 'You only have to look at his father to see where Jorian gets his temper from.'

'But I couldn't do anything,' Darion said. 'Honestly Matt, it really *wasn't* me who started it. It doesn't matter what I do. He hates me anyway.' He stared at the floor. 'No matter what I do,' he said again.

'Then all the more reason to keep out of his way.'

'Oh I'd be glad to do that. Believe me. If he lets me.'

Matt held out a hand towards him, the palm down and fingers spread, to silence him. 'Be careful what you say Darion. Especially here.'

'It's not my fau..'

'That's enough!' All friendship had disappeared from Matthien's voice.

Darion's cheeks went red. He looked away. His great adventure was ruined. The wonderful night was over.

His new friend had got tired of him. It was just like his mother had said after all.

'I am sorry,' Matthien said after a moment. 'But I really do not want you to get into trouble. You're best out of this. Forget everything you've heard tonight. I feel responsible for bringing you here.'

'Here, where I could never belong,' Darion thought. He wanted to storm away, but he was unable to move. It felt as if his feet had grown roots down into the floor.

'It is probably best that you leave,' Matt said. He paused. 'For now anyway. I will see you tomorrow.'

Darion knew it was no good to argue. Without caring now what anyone thought he ran across the room and pushed his way up the stairs towards the doors. A cheer and the sound of laughter behind him made him turn at the last moment. It was clear that the games had begun. All around the hall guests were sipping the liquid from the vials, pointing and laughing with each other. In spite of himself he stopped to watch. Some hunched over and growled threateningly, making their nearby companions flinch back in fear. Others appeared to grow taller, or stronger and more muscled for a few moments. A mixture of tweeting sounds, roars and squeaks joined the party sounds of laughter and conversation as the potions in the bottles did their work. In spite of what he knew about vials and essences, it all seemed so unreal, so different and far away from his real life.

'I don't fit in here,' he thought. 'I wish I'd spent the evening with Vershan instead.'

Just as he turned away to leave, he caught sight of Alianna floating into the air, laughing delightedly, her arms spread wide. Jorian stood close by, looking up at her adoringly, his draccen teeth smacking together hungrily.

Creena and the Machine

'He called him what?' asked Vershan.

'A Tenementerra street urchin! Oh Vershan, you should have seen the snot!'

They were sitting on the front step of Vershan's house, about to set off for their next essence hunting lesson. Vershan was listening wide-eyed to Darion's account of the night before. Telling his friend about it had cheered Darion up straightaway.

'Didn't know the people who lived in the Variegatt even *had* snot,' Vershan said. 'I always imagined it was taken away by golden fairies in the night.' He got up and began to dance around, turning on one foot, pretending to pick at grotty noses with his fingers. 'Lovely noses, long noses,' he sang in a high, tweeting voice. 'Fat noses, Variegatt noses. Fairies pick all their noses, collecting the snot, emptying the slime.'

Darion rolled around, laughing along with Vershan.

'What would fairies do with snot?' he giggled.

'Probably weave it into moneybags for all of that golden Variegatt cash?' Vershan replied. 'I don't know how their minds work up there. They're different to us. Maybe they mix the snot with Cittegarre ear wax to make sauce for their pudding. Or catch flies in snotty cobwebs and eat them like raisins.'

'Snot for cobwebs? Euch! You're disgusting.'

'You started it.'

'Only telling you what I saw.'

'Wish I'd been there,' said Vershan.

Their laughter subsided. Darion started to think about being sent away from the party. He remembered Matthien's hard words.

'Me too,' he said. 'Would've been more fun with you there.'

'I'd have watched your back too,' said Vershan. 'I won't have a Variegatt bully threaten my friends like that.'

'Even if his dad is one of the High Lords of Beltheron?'

'Even then.'

'You sure?'

'To the death!'

'*Really* sure?'

'Well, maybe not. Not to the *death*. No point being stupid about these things.'

They both grinned and burst out laughing again. After a few moments, Vershan went quiet. Darion saw that the smile on his face had gone.

'Seriously though,' said Vershan. 'If he does cause you trouble just let me know, alright?'

Darion nodded. 'Alright.'

Vershan jumped to his feet. 'Now come on, otherwise we'll be late for class and Cleve Harrow will have your snot to make cobwebs.'

*   *   *   *

Their first class that morning was a brand new experiment. Harrow had already begun to speak as Vershan and Darion squeezed into their places. His eyes looked at them disapprovingly for a moment before he continued.

'The essence of your creature can be used as a cure for a variety of ills and diseases,' he said. 'But many believe it can also be useful as an aid to sharpening our senses, improving our own abilities.'

'*Or just to provide a bit of fun and games for the Variegatt lords,*' Darion said to himself. He was still thinking about last night's party, and the way the wealthy guests had used the essences. His mind kept coming back to the image of Alianna, actually *floating* into the air.

'You will remember my lesson a couple of weeks ago,' Cleve Harrow continued. 'You will recall how we used the essence of the far-seeing eagle to produce a potion which made our own eyesight much clearer for several minutes.' The children all nodded. That had been a good lesson. After using the essence, Darion had looked out of the window and been able to see every detail of the small tar-finch birds who were feeding far down at the opposite end of the courtyard.

'Today,' Harrow went on, 'we will concentrate on the feathers of the corvids.'

'The what, sir?' Vershan asked.

'Corvids, boy. Crows, ravens, daws. All have great intelligence and cunning. In fact, in comparison with the actual size of their brains, they are possibly the most intelligent, cunning creatures on the planet.'

There were murmurs of disbelief and laughter around the class.

'You don't believe me?' said Harrow. 'I will show you.'

He moved to a curtained alcove at one side of his desk. Gently, he opened the curtain and made a soft cooing sound. Darion heard a flapping, then a squawk, as a large black raven flew from the shadows and onto Cleve Harrow's outstretched arm.

The laughter in the class turned to gasps of delight.

'Harrow has a pet!'

'He's beautiful.'

'Look at his wings.'

'He's a bit scary. That beak's huge!'

'Careful. He'd have your eyes out in a second if you got too close!'

With the raven still on his arm, Harrow raised his other hand to silence them. The raven stared around the room, taking everyone in. Its head dropped slightly to one side, as if it were considering what to do.

'Class, you have all seen birds such as this on most days of your lives,' Harrow said. 'But you have probably never observed them properly, or even given them a second thought.'

'What did he call them again?' Vershan whispered. 'Crowvids?'

'Corvids. Sshh.'

'Quiet at the back,' barked Harrow. 'There is nothing wrong with my eyes Melgardes. I do not have to rub a farseeing potion of eagle essence onto them to see you talking to Mister Fley.'

'Sir, sorry sir,' the boys chorused together.

Harrow lowered his voice and whispered to the bird. It gave a squawk and flew from his arm onto a perch at the end of his desk.

'Did it just understand what he said to it?' Vershan whispered quietly to Darion.

'She probably understands me more than you do most of the time, Vershan Fley,' Harrow replied. 'There's nothing wrong with my ears either.'

The crow began walking back and forth along the perch. Its head bobbed up and down and tilted to one side again as it continued looking around at the students.

'Ears, ears,' it squawked.

'It can talk!' said Korellia.

'Creena here can mimic several sounds,' Harrow answered. 'I am not sure if she can actually speak in conversation. But I am convinced she understands just about everything I say. Now watch closely.'

The class leaned forwards. Everyone held their breath.

'Creena, would you please kindly fetch me a grape.'

The bird bobbed her head once more for a moment, then spread her wings and flew low over the students' heads. At the far side of the classroom, a bowl of fruits sat on the window-ledge. There were grapes, apples, some cherries still on their stalks, and soft, dark orange apricots. Creena landed carefully on the edge of the bowl and looked in. She considered for a moment then plunged her beak into the bowl.

Picking out a grape in her beak she flew back to Harrow. Landing on his shoulder she dropped it into his waiting hand.

'Could she get me a cherry sir?' Vershan said.

Harrow stared at him hard for a moment.

Creena gave a squawk. 'Ask nice, ask nice,' she said.

The class erupted into a roar of disbelieving laughter. Harrow smiled.

'Perhaps she *can* converse after all, Master Fley. You had better do as she says.'

'Ask nice, say please,' the crow squawked again.

Vershan's face had turned red, but he laughed along with the rest of them.

'Apologies, Creena, please would you be so kind as to fetch me a cherry?'

'Squawk! Better! Better!' Off she flew to the bowl again and returned to Vershan with a red cherry in her beak. He flinched sideways as she landed on his shoulder then held out his hand for the fruit. Creena deliberately squeezed the cherry with her beak and a thin jet of red juice squirted out and down Vershan's face. The class burst into laughter again.

'Enough of this.' Harrow raised a hand to his mouth to hide his own grin and quickly became business-like once more. 'I think this has proved my point about the intelligence of these birds.'

Murmurs of agreement went around the room. Only one hand went up to disagree. It was Sallion, a serious looking boy at the front who always seemed to have more questions than any of the others. 'But sir, you could argue that she is only responding to a handful of very simple commands.'

'Rubbish!' Vershan replied. 'You heard her. She *talked* to me. Huh, she even told me off!'

There was another flutter of giggles from the others.

'Again, just a few words that the Cleve could have taught her,' Sallion went on. 'She might just be responding to a tone of voice in a way that she has been told to.'

'Sallion Targ, that is a good point,' said Harrow. 'And you are quite right to question what I have told you. It is true that Creena here might have been programmed by me to make a fool of our friend Fley here.' Harrow's eyes twinkled with mischief. 'It would be very tempting to get her to do that. But now let me show you that she can in fact use reason, and can even solve problems.'

He reached under his desk and brought out a steel and silver machine.

It was built into a square box just over a metre long on each side. Tubes and levers stuck out at odd angles from every side, and there were flaps and openings in a number of places. You could see clearly through a glass plate which covered one side of the box. Looking inside it, the students saw that the box had been separated into different compartments. These were all connected by either trapdoors, tubes or gates.

At one end Darion and Vershan could see there was a small bowl of nuts and seeds.

At the opposite end to the seeds, a funnel had been attached. Harrow lifted the whole contraption carefully and placed it next to Creena's perch. The perch had a metal cup at one end. Harrow adjusted it so that the funnel was directly over the metal cup.

'There are a number of puzzles here to solve,' he told them. 'A peg to pull out in one place, a knotted string to untie in another, maybe a drawer to open somewhere else. All these must be done in a particular order for the puzzle to move the nuts and seeds through the different compartments and finally drop its reward of food into Creena's cup.'

They all craned their necks once more to get a better view. 'You will have noticed those large objects under the black sheets on the tables at the back of the class. They are exact copies of this contraption. Divide one machine between every four of you. Set up on tables one to five,' he told them.

They all began to split up into their usual working groups, and fetched the boxes onto their own desks.

'Your challenge is a simple one,' said Harrow when the machines were all in place. 'In your normal working teams of four, can you solve the puzzles in the right order to release the food *before* Creena here does?'

An amount of jeering answered this. Of course they could! They were all far more intelligent than a crow, even if it did have better manners than Vershan Fley.

'Very well,' said Harrow. 'Let us find out. There will be a prize for whoever is fastest. You may now begin.'

Creena's Game

They all set about their task excitedly. They pulled the
black covers off the puzzles and the groups huddled
around, poking and prodding at the levers and switches.

Darion and Vershan were in the same group. They worked
with Korellia and another girl, Livia, who was already
scribbling away at a diagram of the machine in her notepad.

'Let's be methodical about this,' she said. Her tongue was
sticking out of the side of her mouth in concentration as she
glanced at her drawing.

'Methodical?' Vershan answered. 'It's obvious where to
start.' He reached forwards and pulled one of the small
levers. There was a clang and a metal plate immediately
dropped down, fixing itself neatly in front of the handles
to two of the other drawers. Now it was impossible to get
at them at all.

'Careful Versh,' said Darion. 'We could have reached in
and opened those a moment ago.'

'Fool!' Korellia said. 'Didn't you see the lever was holding
that metal plate up?'

Vershan frowned. 'I thought...'

'No you didn't,' Korellia replied. 'You didn't think at all,
that's the problem.'

'That's where we start,' said Livia. She pointed at her
diagram, then raised her pencil and gestured towards the

same place on the machine. 'If we untie that string first on the left hand side, it releases that bar holding the first box in place. Then we can move it sideways and get to the handle.'

Darion looked where she was pointing. 'Makes sense,' he said. 'Let's do it.'

Livia was right and soon they had released a small cluster of seeds and raisins from the first box. The seeds ran down a tube into the second box. Now they could begin solving the next part of the problem.

'How are the others doing?' Korellia asked, intent on trying to figure out what the second stage was.

Vershan looked at the other tables.

'Bedellya and her cronies on table four have only just started,' he said. 'She's busy scribbling down notes. But Serious Sallion seems to have taken over on table three. He's bossing everyone around and they're already onto the third box. Table one and five look to be doing about as well as us and...' There was another clang and a wail of frustration from Sallion as the metal plate fell down over the doors in the same way as it had on their own machine.

'Heh, Serious Sallion isn't as clever as he thinks; he made the same mistake as me,' Vershan grinned.

'But look at Creena,' Darion said. 'She isn't doing anything.'

They all glanced over to watch the bird. It seemed that Darion was right. She was simply looking at the machine, her head cocked to one side, as if unable to decide what to do.

'Useless thing,' Vershan said. 'She can't do anything after all.'

'Don't be too sure,' Livia replied as she went back to studying her diagrams. 'She's being methodical, like me.'

'Whatever she's thinking, we need to get a move on ourselves,' said Korellia. 'Look at them over on table five.'

There was certainly a buzz of excited activity on the far side of the room. The students at table five had got as far as the last box, where a cam needed to be turned. This would lift up the final box to tip its contents into the funnel. They had almost solved it, but it seemed that they hadn't spotted how the cam turned yet.

'If only you hadn't dropped the metal plate,' Korellia complained. 'We might have got there by now.'

'It's ok,' said Darion. He had been looking at the problem on his own for a few moments. 'I think I can see a way around it.'

He pointed at the metal plate that had blocked the drawers when Vershan had released it. It fitted snugly into a frame. It was so tight that they could not get their fingers in to lift it back up again. But Darion had noticed a small hole under one end of the frame. If he could push through that with something narrow enough, they could lever the plate out of the way and get on with the last part of the puzzle.

'Livia, give me your pencil,' he said.

'What?'

'Don't argue. Quickly, your pencil.'

She handed it to him.

'Don't snap the point,' she warned him. 'It takes me ages to get it as sharp as I want it.'

He took no notice and managed to push it through the hole. Twisting it around, Darion worked the metal plate high enough to get his fingers underneath it. Vershan and Korellia saw what he was doing and reached forwards to help. In a moment they had lifted the top of the plate, which Darion had now levered free of the frame. Out it came and Livia, who had already worked out the next part, turned the cam to lift the final box.

'Hurry,' Darion said. 'It looks as if Creena's finally worked it out.'

Sure enough Creena was now flapping about on Harrow's table. Her wings fluttered as she manoeuvred herself to different points of the machine, pecking and pulling. Her claws grabbed at buttons and switches as her beak pulled levers. After taking her time at the beginning, she was now working with furious speed. It seemed unbelievable, but the bird was catching them up!

They turned their attention back to their own machine.

'Come on, Livia, hurry!'

Livia gave another turn of the cam and their last box tilted sufficiently to tip the food.

'We've done it!' Darion yelled. The seeds and nuts dropped from the final box into the funnel.

'Catch them,' said Vershan, plunging his hands under the spout.

'Well done everyone,' Korellia said. 'We've won.'

'I don't think so,' Livia replied. 'Look.'

She pointed at Harrow's table. They all turned around. Even as their raisins and seeds dropped into Vershan's cupped hands, they saw Creena already pecking away happily at those in her own cup. Every part of her puzzle had been solved perfectly.

'I was watching closely,' Harrow told them. 'She finished three whole seconds before you did. The prize goes to Creena.'

There was a groan from the students. They stared at the crow with disbelief.

'Creena won, Creena won, Creena won,' she cawed happily.

The Experiment

'Creena, my friend, would you please allow me to take some of the small, soft feathers from under your wing?'

'Squawk!'

'Won't it hurt her, sir?' Korellia asked.

'Not a bit, she will often groom herself and pick out the older feathers that are about to moult anyway. We'll just take a few of those.'

Creena was already preening herself and plucking under her wings at some of the black downy fluff. It seemed to come away quite easily and soon she had made a small pile of feathers on the desk.

'Thank you my dear, that will be enough.'

Creena flew back up onto her perch and pecked at some more of her seeds in the metal cup.

Harrow began placing the feathers into his beautiful grey and silver essence jar. 'Gather around,' he called to the class. 'You need to make a note of how much essence oil is added for each feather before we stir in the transforming liquid.'

They all pushed back their chairs and formed a huddle around his desk. There was no chatter now. Since his defensive action against the brannoch and his admission about being a mage, the Cleve had commanded much more respect amongst his students. Even Vershan was intent upon what Harrow was about to do next.

Using a small oval measuring jug, Harrow poured the thick liquid into the jar until it had covered most of the feathers.

'Imagine all of that intelligence you have just witnessed, coming from such a tiny brain,' he said. 'Think of that reasoning multiplied by the size and functioning of our own brainpower. This is what essencing is all about. Giving us the chance to be as clever, as swift, as courageous or as hardworking as we can be. Clever as our friend Creena here. Swift as a silkefox, courageous as an ur-lion, or as hardworking, focused and dedicated as that bee buzzing around the flowers there.' He pointed to a jar of bright red blooms near to the window of the classroom. A bee was just backing out of one of the flower heads, its legs thick and sticky with pollen.

Harrow drew their attention back to his own work.

'The effects of this essencing are not permanent of course. No one has yet discovered the next stage of the process: the one which will allow us to make that permanent change to our personalities.'

Darion remembered what Alianna had told him about the game at the party. If you took some of the liquid, it allowed you to mimic behaviour, or adopt a creature's skills for a few moments, but the experience was soon over. He wondered what it would be like to choose to have the strength of a pedjiaar, or to have Creena's quick wits, and to keep them forever.

His thoughts were interrupted by an angry shout from across the room.

'Steady!' There was a loud crash. 'Ohh, now look what you've done!'

Darion turned. The shout had come from Korellia. Livia had knocked over one of the heavy containers filled with the transforming liquid. It had splashed all over the front of Korellia's smock and was running in thick rivulets down the sides of the desk.

'What in the name of the seers is going on over there?' Harrow bellowed across at them.

Livia's cheeks had turned deep red. Korellia stared at the class indignantly.

'It wasn't me sir,' Korellia began. 'I was just...'

'Enough!' Harrow cut her short. 'I am not apportioning any blame. Accidents will happen. Unfortunately this one is particularly annoying. My supplies are running short. Vershan Fley, go and look in my store room to see if there is another jar.'

'Yes sir,' Vershan began to run across the room.

'Slowly, Fley, and carefully,' the Cleve warned. 'Do not be the cause of further breakages. You mustn't hurry.'

'Sir, no sir. Empty shelf sir. You need to go get some more. Shall I put a note in your shopping bag sir?'

There were a few giggles around the room. Harrow silenced it easily by raising his hand.

'There is no need for a shopping list, Fley' he said. 'But if that is indeed the last of the transforming liquid I do need to send someone on an errand. Melgardes,' he said to Darion. 'There is nothing smart in just standing there gawping and grinning at your friend's foolishness. If you have nothing better to do then you can go to Gretton Tur's workshop for me.' Harrow began scribbling a note and thrust it into Darion's hands. 'Tell him we need another litre of this before this afternoon.'

'Sir, yes sir.'

'And Melgardes?' Harrow continued.

'Sir?'

'You *can* hurry. After the brannoch attack of yesterday there have already been enough delays in everyone's studies this week.'

'Right away Cleve.'

As he began to get up, a sudden thought came to Darion. An opportunity had just presented itself to replace his broken jar. He knew that Gretton Tur's chambers and workshop were filled with all sorts of bottles, jars and other essencing equipment. While he was on his errand for Harrow, Darion could pretend that one of the classroom's essencing jars had also been smashed. He could ask for more liquid and a new jar at the same time! The classroom jars were not bound by the same rules as those given to the students. He knew that occasionally they had to be replaced, and that this was done out of college funds. He couldn't remember Harrow asking for any new ones for ages, so it would be quite believable to want one now. Darion realised that it would mean lying. There was a huge risk of getting found out and punished later, but everyone knew that Gretton Tur was very secretive. He kept himself to himself and hardly ever talked to other people. It was unlikely that he would discuss the conversation with anyone else. Darion was already planning what he would say to ask for a new jar as he grabbed his bag and hurried to the door.

Livia had gone into a sulk as he walked past her desk. Korellia was still looking grumpy as she tried to wipe the spilt transforming potion off her smock.

*   *   *   *

He moved quickly down the corridor towards Tur's rooms. Students rarely got a chance to see inside this part of the building. Tur hated most people's company – that of the students most of all.

Harrow often told them to leave Gretton Tur in peace. He said that the old man was involved in important study and didn't like to be interrupted. This was fine with Darion, Vershan and their classmates. Tur scared them. There was something very odd about the way he scuttled around the corridors of the great halls. Rumours abounded about who he really was. Some said that he was hundreds of years old; others whispered suspicions that he wasn't even human. But this was just stupid gossip. Darion knew that the people who said things like that were only trying to tease and scare the new students. He had learnt long ago that you couldn't believe everything that people told you.

As he approached the door to Gretton Tur's study it opened and Tur himself stepped out into the corridor. Every time Darion saw him he shuddered. It wasn't the grey wrinkles of his skin that flaked around his mouth, or the huddled, shuffling way Tur moved that always made him look like a reptile. No, the thing that turned Darion's blood cold in his veins was the look in Tur's eyes. They were covered by a thin, milky film, and he always felt that the old man could see right into his thoughts.

Those eyes turned on Darion now as he almost bumped into him.

'Dullard,' Tur said to him. 'Be more careful, you worthless shred.'

Darion bowed. 'I'm sorry, my lord.'

'What do you want?'

Darion showed him the note that Harrow had given him. 'A message sir, from the Cleve, sir.'

Tur's hand extended impatiently from under his thick shawl. 'Give it to me then.' His fingers flicked and twitched at the paper in Darion's hand. It was like the last jerking movements of a dying bird's wing.

Darion handed over the paper. Tur looked briefly at it and grunted. 'Very well, I will send some today.'

'And.. and,' Darion steeled himself, plucking up the courage to begin the lie that he had practised in his head. 'And we need another essence jar becau...'

Gretton Tur waved him away.

'I'm too busy right now. If it escaped your notice, boy, we were attacked by a brannoch yesterday. Another assault could happen at any moment. I have important consultations to make.'

In spite of himself, Darion wanted to say: 'I know all about the brannoch sir, I saw it, we all did, we saw it up close.' But Tur began to turn away. As he did he thrust the note back into Darion's fingers.

'Push this under my door. I will deal with it when I return.'

'But the new jar...'

'I said I will deal with it later!'

'Sir, yes sir.' Darion felt foolish. Why could he never sound intelligent in front of the elders? How would they ever take him seriously, how would he ever change and become an important essence hunter, or a pulver like his father, if all he could do was mutter, 'Sir, yes sir,' like a fool.

Tur was already disappearing around the corner of the corridor. Darion knew that the old man had forgotten about him already.

There was nothing for it. His plan to get a new jar had failed. Darion sighed and bent down to push Cleve Harrow's message under the door. He put his hand against it to balance himself. As he did the latch clicked and the door swung open slightly. It hadn't been fastened properly. Tur had forgotten to lock it! Darion froze. He didn't move for several seconds. All of his instincts told him to reach up to the handle and pull the door closed again. That was the safe thing to do. That was the right thing to do. *'Just close the door and walk away, Darion,'* he thought to himself. *'Close it and walk away now.'* But still he didn't move.

Darion looked around. There was no one else in the corridor. His fingers were already touching the door handle. This was madness! He paused and listened. He couldn't hear any footsteps. There were no voices. Holding his breath he stood up slowly. Darion made his way on tiptoe to the bend in the corridor where Tur had gone. Edging forwards he peered around the corner. The hallway stretched out in front of him for some distance. Tur was already out of sight.

Darion thought frantically. He was desperate to look inside Tur's room, but he knew the dreadful trouble he would be in if he were discovered. *'You're in enough of a mess already,'* he told himself. *'As if it's not enough that you've broken the most valuable thing you own – and are ever likely to own – and daren't even own up to it.'*

Still he waited. He chewed his lip hard, trying to make his decision. He knew he would never get a chance like this again. He couldn't help thinking about how impressed Vershan would be - and how jealous - when he found out. He still couldn't hear a sound. No one was coming. It would only take a moment. Just a quick look wouldn't do any harm. There might be a jar right there, within arm's reach! *'If I stay near to the door I can run back out again in a second if I hear anyone,'* he thought.

That was it. He knew he was going to do it. Moving swiftly back to the door he pushed it open a bit more. With one final glance to left and right - still no one coming – he stepped inside Tur's room.

The Workshop

D arion quickly closed the door behind him. As he took his fingers from the handle he noticed that the key had been left in the lock on the inside. Tur must have been in a real hurry to leave. For a moment Darion considered locking himself in while he explored the room, but immediately realised how crazy this would be. 'That's right, why not trap yourself in here,' he murmured. 'That would be really smart.' He left the key where it was.

Harrow's note was still in his hand. He considered it for a moment then placed it on the floor just inside the door. He looked at it, and moved it backwards and forwards a couple of times. Soon he was satisfied that it looked as if he had pushed it under the door from outside. He stood again and turned back to Tur's chamber.

The morning sunlight streamed in through a tall window at one end of the room. It gave enough light for him to see clearly as he looked around at the details of Tur's workshop. There were shelves everywhere. Most of them were lined two or three deep with books and folders bursting with papers. Others were stacked with a clutter of bottles, pieces of measuring equipment, vials and tubing. Darion had never seen such a room. It would take him a lifetime to work his way through even a fraction of those books, he thought. He couldn't even guess what some of the mechanical equipment might be used for.

He began to move slowly through the room, gazing around open mouthed.

A huge tapestry hung on the wall at the opposite end of the room. It was the only part of the workshop walls not covered by shelves. The tapestry swept from the ceiling all the way down to the floor. It was faded in places, but Darion could still see flashes of bright colours here and there. He stepped closer and saw that it showed a hunting scene. Grey robed riders held spears high above their heads as their horses bore down upon a weird creature. It was shaped like a dog, but reared up on its hind legs. Instead of fur it seemed to be covered in a slippery grey skin, like a lizard. Darion reckoned that it must be at least the size of a fully grown man. Its eyes blazed furiously out of the tapestry. 'Looks as angry as Beskar next door,' he grinned. Then his face fell. The creature in the tapestry also looked a little bit like a brannoch. He shivered.

He hadn't come in here just to look at an old tapestry though. Darion began to make his way along the shelves. Row upon row of dusty volumes passed before his eyes. Around the corner was a workbench. Above it was a high shelf. He couldn't see what was on it but there was a small brass plate screwed to the edge. He peered more closely at it and read the words 'essence jars.' He had found them! He raised himself up onto his toes and peered over the edge. Lined up on this shelf were dozens and dozens of jars. They were all different shapes and sizes but one of them caught his attention immediately. It was behind a couple of shorter bottles, towards the back. It was about twenty five centimetres high with a long, wide neck opening onto a broad, circular bowl at its base. His heart leapt. It was roughly the same shape and size as his! Not only that, the colours on the glass were almost identical too. It swirled with pale greens and blues.

This was even better than he had hoped. Why not just swap it! There were so many other bottles and containers here that it would be months before Tur noticed the change. If he *ever* did. Most of the jars were so dusty and neglected that Darion knew it must be years since Tur had used them, or even looked at them closely. What amazing luck. Now he didn't even have to ask Tur for a replacement as he had planned. All he had to do was take this matching one and leave his own in its place. His problems would be over and he needn't worry about it anymore. At first the relief was so great that he laughed out loud. His hands were already in his rucksack, scrabbling around for his jar.

He lifted it out. Going up on tiptoe again he reached up to the shelf. He stretched out to move the shorter jars out of the way. But that was as far as he could reach. He could just about get his fingers onto the jar he needed, but it was impossible to grab hold of it. Darion stepped back and looked at the workbench underneath. It looked strong enough to hold his weight. Placing his palms on it he pulled himself up. Now he could easily reach up and get his hand around the neck of the jar. The workbench groaned under him and he started to sweat in fear. But sure enough it held his weight. In a moment he had the jar tightly in his fingers. Breathlessly he took it down. Holding both jars up to the light from the window he compared them. He had been right; the two jars were the same size and shape. Only by a close examination would anyone notice the slight difference in the way the colours changed their shade from green to blue. Even better, if he put his own jar on the shelf and moved the shorter ones back in front of it, they would hide the worst of the cracks. He was certain that it would be hard to spot the difference. This was going to be easy!

Darion reached back up once more to leave his own jar on the dusty shelf. Then he stopped. What he was doing was wrong, he knew that. Most people would call it stealing, and he didn't want to think of himself as a thief. He paused and held the two jars side by side.

. He looked at them for several moments then gave a deep sigh. A memory of his father sprang up in his imagination and he knew that he would never forgive such a thing. His father had been the most honest man Darion had ever known. He didn't want to betray his memory by stealing. He *couldn't*.

Then in his imagination, he heard Vershan's voice. *'Don't be stupid! It's not as if anyone's getting hurt is it? Just take it and you'll be out of trouble.'*

This voice made sense. Would anyone really get hurt? Was it *really* stealing if he left his own in return? The jar obviously hadn't been used, or even moved, for months. Once again he began to convince himself that it was alright. What difference would it make to Tur? He would never even miss the jar. And it would make all the difference in the world to Darion.

Then he heard a rustling, scraping sound outside the door. Seer's blood, he had stayed there too long! There was a dull thud from the corridor, as if someone had dropped a bag onto the floor. Then he heard a grumbling voice. 'Where is it? Where did I put it?' It was Tur's voice. He had come back! There was more grumbling. What was Tur doing? In a moment, Darion understood. The old man was searching his pockets for the key that Darion had discovered still in the lock.

As quickly and quietly as he could, Darion placed Tur's jar back on the shelf. His mind had been made up for him; if he was going to be discovered, at least he wouldn't be holding Tur's property in his hands. If he had to, he could talk his way out of being in the room. He had an excuse after all. He had been sent on an errand by the Cleve. He could even go back to his original idea of asking for a replacement jar for the classroom.

But as he was thinking about how he would ask for the jar, he heard Tur cursing again outside the door: 'If that young wretch of Harrow's hadn't interrupted me, I would have... graah ! The next time I see his worthless face I'll put out his tongue!'

Darion's courage failed him. The thought of Tur's anger drove everything else out of his mind. He knew he couldn't face him. All he cared about now was getting out without being seen. Quickly placing his own jar back in his rucksack he dropped down from the workbench to the floor. Scuttling silently to the end of a row of shelves, he squeezed into a narrow gap between them.

He only just managed to hide before the door opened. Darion peered out between the two tall bookcases and saw Tur close the door again behind him. He reached down to the lock and tutted to himself as he discovered the key, still in place. 'Huh,' Darion overheard him mutter. 'Minutes ago you were teasing that boy about being foolish. Look at you yourself. You're no better!'

Tur closed the door behind him and locked it. Darion held his breath. He felt his skin prickle with fright. If Tur took the key with him now, he would be trapped. *'Idiot!'* he scolded himself. *'Why didn't you take the key yourself?'*

But then he saw Tur turn away, leaving the key in the lock. Darion gave a huge sigh of relief. He carried on watching. The old man bent down and picked up Harrow's note from the floor where Darion had placed it. Then he made his way across the room. He passed by on the other side of the shelves where Darion was hiding. He was so close that the boy could smell the musty cloak that he wore.

Tur paused by the tapestry and looked around. Darion shrank back further into the shadow of the bookcase.

Tur's eyes roved around the room. Then he turned back and pulled the tapestry to one side. Darion could now see a doorway behind it. Tur fumbled at the lock of this door for a moment then glanced around again. He took one more look around the room, opened the door and ducked through. From his hiding place Darion could just make out the room beyond. He waited several moments. He could hear the mage moving around in this second chamber.

Darion knew that there were dozens of hidden rooms or annexes like this throughout the buildings in the great halls. His father had told him about the labyrinth of tunnels that ran underneath the city. They had been there for centuries, his father said. Now most of the hidden rooms they led to were used for storage. Sometimes the masters used them as sleeping quarters when they were working late. Darion also remembered what Matthien had told him about the dungeons running for miles under the earth. Is that what *this* door led to?

The boy twisted around and looked back towards the main door that would lead him back into the hallway and safety. He would have to cross Tur's whole study to get there. Tur only had to look around at the wrong moment, or come back in from the second room and he would be discovered.

Darion knew he was panicking again. He knew he had to think straight to get himself out of this. His eyes searched around frantically and noticed that there was another high book shelf at one end of Tur's main desk. It was directly opposite the open doorway to the room where Tur had disappeared. It might just block him from view as he made his way to the door. Darion thought that he could make it to that bookshelf in three strides. Then it should be an easy dash to the main door and he could escape without being seen.

But Darion's curiosity got the better of him. He wanted to know what Tur was doing. When he got to that high bookshelf he could risk looking into the far room to see what was going on. If Tur was near to the doorway and Darion was in danger of being discovered, he could just stay hidden until the old man turned away again or moved further into the second room.

Breathlessly Darion moved from his hiding place. He could hear the sounds of Tur's movements quite clearly.

Stepping out quickly, Darion crept across the floor. He placed his feet carefully so as not to make a sound on the hard slates. In a moment he had made his way to the edge of the high bookcase. So far so good. Darion now risked a look back past the tapestry and through the doorway into the second room.

Inside, Tur was standing with his back to him. He was bending over a heavy leather volume. It rested on an old wooden lectern. Darion carried on watching Tur for a moment as he pored over the pages of the book. He knew it was too risky to stay any longer. He turned to leave.

Then a small noise caught his attention. At first he thought that Tur had coughed, or cleared his throat. Then he heard the sound again. It was coming from another part of Tur's second room, a part that Darion couldn't see. This time he could tell that it wasn't a cough. It was more like a growl. He turned back once more, holding his breath.

Knowing how dangerous his situation was, he stepped towards the room. As he got closer to the gap in the tapestry, he could see the corner of a table next to where Tur stood. There was a thick rope running down from the edge of the table to a metal ring bolted to the floor. Darion saw the rope twitch as it was pulled tight. At the same moment he heard the growl again.

'Hush hush,' Tur said. 'Lie still, it will all be over in a moment.'

Darion froze in horror as Tur moved from his lectern and approached the table. He was still turned away from

Darion, but the boy glimpsed a glass tube in the old mage's hand. The tube was filled with a yellow liquid.

Tur disappeared from view as he moved around the table. Darion heard the growling growing more frantic. The length of rope pulled more tightly against the metal ring once more and then went still.

'This time, my pretty, this time.' Tur's voice had taken on a sickly edge of fake sweetness that turned Darion's stomach.

'Lie still, *that's* the way,' Tur cooed. Darion daren't take another step forwards to see more of the room, but as he watched the corner of the table, there was another unexpected movement. A tail twitched into view. A grey and red striped tail. Tur had a pedjiaar strapped to the table!

There was a sudden enraged roar, followed by a frightened, squealing yelp. The rope jerked. The tail drooped. Then silence. Darion was frozen. His eyes and mouth wide open in horror.

'Seer's bloody talons!' cursed Tur. 'The essence be damned!'

Darion heard him move swiftly around the table and then saw him back at the lectern, engrossed in the old book again. Vile words still hissed through his teeth. He turned the pages with a violent flick of his hand.

Darion stared from his hiding place. He swallowed hard, trying to get a tight lump of fear out of his throat. What had he just witnessed? Whatever it was he was mad to still be in here! If Tur spotted him now, spying on him, he would be in *really* serious trouble. Spying was a crime; he could go to prison! With a shudder that brought him back to his senses, he started to edge backwards towards the door. The only thing he wanted to do now was to get out without being caught. If he could reach the corridor before the mage turned around then he could hurry straight back to the class, his message from Harrow delivered and no one would be any the wiser.

With his heart pumping so heavily in his chest he feared that Gretton Tur must be able to hear it, Darion increased his stride towards the door. His hand out in front of him, he reached for the key. Don't scrape in the lock, please don't get stuck!

Shifting his rucksack into a more secure place on his shoulder, he gripped the key with one hand he twisted it and turned the handle with the other. Thankfully, it opened without a sound.

Feeling sick, Darion hurried through into the corridor. He closed the door again behind him. His luck held. The corridor was empty. There was no one to witness his escape from Tur's study.

He started to run, the rucksack bouncing against his side. *'Steady Darry, steady,'* he told himself.

Rounding a corner, he slowed again, and in a few more paces brought himself back to normal walking speed. No one who saw him now would guess at the danger he had just faced. Even his heartbeat began to slow again. His mind still raced though, filled with questions about what he had seen.

Whatever Tur had been doing in that room, Darion knew that it must be a dreadful secret. He remembered the way Tur had glanced around before opening the door. He had seen evil in Tur's eyes at that moment, but there was something else as well. What was it? Guilt? Shame perhaps? No, neither of those things. Darion understood that furtive look hiding in Tur's eyes. It was fear. Gretton Tur was *afraid* of being discovered. Darion gulped hard at the questions racing through his head. Why would such a powerful mage be afraid? What might he do to keep such a secret? And what would he do to silence anyone who discovered it?

The Wrong Jar

Darion had almost reached the school buildings and Cleve Harrow's classroom. About to enter the courtyard, he stopped dead in his tracks. A cold wave of horror washed over him; a sudden suspicion that he had made an awful mistake. Darion tried to remember exactly what he had done in those last desperate moments before Tur had come back into his study. He went over it all again in his head, bit by bit. When he heard Tur returning, he had panicked. He had placed one jar back on the shelf, and then put the other in his rucksack. But he had been in a dreadful hurry. He hadn't looked at what he was doing. He hadn't checked the jars. Even though he was in a rush, not thinking properly, surely he wouldn't have been so stupid as to...? No! He couldn't have...!

Cursing at himself, he reached up and unslung his rucksack from his shoulder.

Feeling down inside it, he felt the essence jar. His fingers closed around it and he felt the smooth, curved surface.

Smooth.

No cracks.

He closed his eyes and groaned. After all of that arguing with his conscience he had put the wrong jar back on Gretton Tur's shelf. He had ended up stealing the other one anyway!

Darion slumped down against the wall and lifted out Tur's jar. He took a proper look at it. It was so much like his own there was no wonder he had got them mixed up.

Darion gave a short, bitter laugh to himself.

There was nothing to do about it now. He had already taken far too long on his errand. Harrow would start to wonder where on earth he was. Darion decided the best thing to do for now would be to act as naturally as possible.

'It will be fine,' he kept on saying to himself. *'Tur will probably never notice.'*

He carried on trying to reassure himself all the way back up to the classroom. But even so, he now knew that Tur held a secret. He knew that if Tur *did* notice the changed jar, and if he suspected someone had been spying on him, then he would not rest until he found them.

Luckily, when Darion got back to his desk, Harrow was busy discussing something with a student at the far side of the class. The rest of the room all had their heads down over their studies. Then Darion's legs turned to water. It wasn't a student Harrow was talking to. It was Matthien. He was the only one who noticed Darion's return. He waved at him as he made his way back to his seat.

'I hope you don't mind me coming here again,' he said. 'I wanted to apologise about my behaviour last night.'

'It's ok,' Darion replied.

'I hope that we can put it behind us?'

'It's fine, really.' He had far too many things to worry about than what had happened at the party.

Cleve Harrow turned towards him. 'Master Melgardes, did you get the mutabar liquid?'

'Tur was busy sir, so I left him your note sir'

'Left it?'

'He was just leaving sir so I pushed it under his door, that's what he told me to do you see and then I...'

Harrow frowned. 'This is really most annoying. Well I suppose it can't be helped.'

Matthien spoke up. 'Tur can be a stubborn goat at times. I can't have your apprentices here held up in their studies. Allow me. I will go to see him myself.'

'My lord,' said Harrow. ' I could not expect you to waste your ti...'

Matthien waved away his objection with his hand.

'Nonsense. No need to worry. Tur provides the Variegatt with so many potions and items, and charges such a high price too, that he won't dare to annoy me. He'll lose far too much business. Believe me I'll have this all sorted out in a slice.'

He turned towards the door. As he did he glanced down at Darion's bag on the desk. He saw the essence jar inside. Before Darion could stop him, Matthien lifted it out. He turned it around in his hands, examining it.

'Oh, that looks good. I'm glad you managed to get it repaired.'

Darion swallowed hard. 'Yes, it, er, it took me some time but it looks fine now.'

'Good as new I'd say,' said Matthien. He paused for a moment and frowned, as if about to say something else. Then he smiled again. 'Yes, good as new. Excellent. I don't like to see a friend in trouble over such a small thing. I'll see you later.'

Darion just nodded dumbly in reply as Matthien left.

Home Again

Thankfully, the rest of the afternoon passed by normally without further incident. By the time he said goodbye to Vershan at his door and continued home, he had begun to put his adventures behind him.

'All of that worry,' he thought. 'And nothing bad happened after all. No one found me out. Another couple of days and everyone will have forgotten that I was even sent to Tur's rooms in the first place.'

But even so, the memory of the pedjiaar strapped to the table, the sight of that cruel looking syringe in Tur's hand, made Darion shiver. There was an echo in his head too, about the snatch of conversation he had overheard at the party. About Argolin and Tur gaining power. The more he considered it the more he convinced himself that it was connected with what he had seen.

He was still wondering about Tur as he rounded the corner into his street. He walked past his neighbour's house, still distracted by what the old mage had been doing. Then he realised there was something different about his street. He slowed down as he drew nearer to his house.

The sun had almost set. By now the city's night-lampers had finished lighting most of the street lamps. But there were none shining near his home. Darion stopped in his tracks. His part of the street was in shadow. But there was something else as well. It wasn't just the darkness which bothered him. It was the fact that the street was silent.

Beskar, his neighbour's dog, hadn't barked.

Darion peered ahead. His eyes searched the gloom around his own house. In the gathering night he could just make out his front door. It was slightly ajar. Out of the darkness he saw a flickering light coming from inside. Then he heard voices.

Darion froze to the spot. Like the cold wind that blows before the arrival of a rainstorm, he felt a shudder of cold run down his spine.

A crash from inside his house made his heart stop. He heard a short scream from just beyond his door. It was cut off quickly and only lasted a moment, but it was enough. He would recognise his mother's voice anywhere.

Darion shrank back into the shadows of his neighbour's doorway. In one corner of his mind he registered that Beskar still didn't bark and that their house was completely dark inside.

He glanced across the street from his hiding place. Still no light shone from any of the houses on that side either. Surely by now someone would have lit a candle?

Then his mother cried out again. It was a cry of someone who had been hurt sharply and suddenly.

He heard a second voice. 'We'll ask you once more. Where is the boy?'

'By the seer's bloody teeth I tell you I don't know!' His mother sounded frantic with terror. But Darion heard a note of outrage in her voice too.

Then she screamed again.

'I tell you, I don't *know* where Darion is!'

Just as he feared. They were looking for *him*.

Tur must have noticed the missing jar after all and guessed that he was the only one who could have taken it.

The people in the house must be Tur's henchmen. They had come to punish him. To get the jar back. To find out what he knew. How could he have been so simple-minded to think that something like this wouldn't happen? Darion's legs buckled under him. The cold chill spread across his shoulder blades and he felt his mouth go dry.

A third cry from his mother pierced his ears. Tears stung his eyes.

'Tell us!'

'Where's the boy?'

He had to own up. He had to save his mother. There was nothing else to do. But still he waited, crouched in the doorway. He squirmed with fear, hating himself, unable to step forwards.

As he hesitated, the door flew wide open. Two burly guards stepped out. They were tall and had to duck down low as they came into the street. Both wore thick hoods. Darion squinted from his hiding place in the shadows of the unlit street, and tried to make out their features. The guards stepped to one side. He saw his mother being pushed out onto the road by someone still inside the house. Only his terror stopped him from crying out loud to see his mother like this. The ropes binding her tightened around her arms as she staggered forwards.

The person holding onto the ropes came out next.

Darion's stomach lurched as he saw this figure. It was shaped like a dog, but stood up on its hind legs. Instead of fur, its body was covered with a scaly, wet looking skin. The head was huge, twice as large as it should have been. It snarled and showed fangs like a wild boar sticking out from both upper and lower jaws. Even in the gloom Darion saw a red glow in its eyes.

The beast cracked the ropes and his mother moved forwards jerkily.

'Come on, Tenementerra filth,' the largest of her captors said. 'We'll soon find out what you know.'

He watched, helpless with terror, as they dragged his mother past his hiding place. She turned for a moment, and saw him cowering in the shadows. Just before she was dragged off her eyes grew wide as she recognised that it was him. His mouth opened to cry out, but she shook her head briefly at him. She just had chance to make a 'shushing' shape with her lips, telling him to keep quiet and stay hidden. Then there was another drag on the rope and they were gone.

The boy sank to his knees and sobbed. Why hadn't he done anything? Why hadn't he helped? He was useless. His father would have saved her. He would have known what to do. But, Darion realised, he was nothing like his father. He was a coward.

After what seemed like a long time he got to his feet. Wiping his nose on his sleeve he made his way towards his house.

He looked in to the living area and saw that a couple of chairs had been turned over. The kitchen fire was still burning and he could smell the stew that his mother had been preparing for supper. The smell of it brought tears to his eyes again. He swallowed hard and went towards his own room. The curtain had been torn to one side, the rings scattered across the floor. His mattress had been overturned and ripped apart. The shelves had been emptied and now all of his books and collections were thrown around, stamped underfoot. Not knowing what else to do he knelt down and started to pick them up. His mother wouldn't want to see such a mess when she got back and...

The sobs rose up in his throat again. What if she *didn't* come back? What if he never saw her again? Sitting on the floor in the middle of the wreckage, he gave himself up to his tears.

The Next Horror

He didn't know how long he lay there, curled up on the floor. It must have been a long time. It was now totally dark outside. Even the various city noises from further away in the Cittegare district had faded into silence. Darion got to his feet. He sniffed and wiped his eyes with the back of his sleeve.

He wondered why the guards had been so violent with his mother. If they wanted to question him why didn't they just turn up at his home and wait for him to come back? Why did they have to take his mother? It wasn't her fault. And why had they brought that horrible scaly creature with them? He shuddered as he thought of it again and it occurred to him that it looked a lot like the creature in the tapestry on Tur's wall. The attack on his house had been so desperate that Darion realised he had been right. Tur needed to keep his experiment with the pedjiaar a secret at any cost. Either that or they obviously needed the stolen essence jar very badly indeed.

He picked up his rucksack and reached inside for it. He held the jar up and looked closely at the smooth rounded object.

He made his decision. He had to take it to them, straight away. He had to confess what he had done, tell them that it was all a silly mistake, and that he hadn't meant to take it. He would tell them that he was really sorry. He hadn't even used the jar, and never meant to keep it. At the same time he would somehow let them know he hadn't noticed anything in the room, that he had been in and out in an instant, that they needn't worry about him. Darion began to run a number of different excuses through his head, trying to decide which one worked best, and what he was going to say to Gretton Tur.

But even as he kept reassuring himself that there was nothing to worry about, that it *had* been a mistake, the thought of the old mage made him groan inside with terror.

Darion knew himself too well. He would never be able to face up to him. No matter how he wished to be like his father, a brave pulver in the service of the city, he knew that he didn't have the courage to do that.

Not alone anyway. He couldn't do it on his own.

Then he thought of his friend.

Vershan. Vershan would help him. He had said as much, only this morning. He had as good as promised. Yes, Vershan would know what to do.

He could go to his friend and ask for his advice. Darion knew that Vershan would even go with him to face Gretton Tur if he asked him.

Once he had come to his decision, Darion didn't hesitate any longer. The thought of his mother being dragged away by Tur's men stabbed at his conscience once more.

Pushing the essence jar back into his rucksack, he set off through the night streets to his friend's house.

*   *   *   *

He heard the commotion before he even turned into Vershan's street. A woman was sobbing and there was an angry, confused argument going on. He picked up his pace and was running by the time he came up to his friend's house. A group of pulver were standing outside the doorway, their familiar pale blue cloaks lit by their torches.

Two of the pulver were questioning a couple of people standing close to Vershan's front door. A little way off, two other men were talking in loud voices, trying to get them to listen to their side of the story. The sobbing woman was being supported by a girl about Darion's age. He recognised both of them. They were Vershan's neighbours. The girl had been in the same class for a short time before he and Vershan had both changed classes to begin their essence hunting studies with Cleve Harrow. He searched his memory for her name; Reanna? Oleander? No, that wasn't right. Then, as he drew closer, he remembered. Larena, that was it.

'What's happened?' he asked as he approached.

Larena looked up. Her eyes were red and her cheeks damp with tears.

'Darion, oh Darion, it's horrible.'

He looked at the two pulver, and then towards the front door. His heart sank and he thought he would be sick as he saw a glimpse of the wreckage within.

'What's happened, Larena?' he repeated.

She sniffed and her voice came out in short bursts. 'We don't know. No one does. They're asking questions. Over there. The two pulver. But no one saw anything.'

One of the pulver had seen him and moved towards them.

'Who are you?' he asked Darion.

Darion was about to tell them, when he thought better of it. Instead of giving his name he just told the guard that he was a friend of the boy who lived there.

'Did you know him well?'

The word 'did" shot into his chest like a dagger. *Did* you know him. Not *do* you know him. Did. *Did.* The word swam around Darion's head until it lost any sense or meaning.

112

Did.

Did.

DID you know him?

He felt dizzy and his legs turned to water…

*   *   *   *

'Boy. Boy? Are you alright?'

The pulver was standing over him. For some reason Darion found himself lying on the ground. Larena was crouching down next to him. Her hand was on his arm.

'Darion? Darion! Are you alright? I think you just fainted.'

He felt other hands helping him to his feet.

'What happened?' His voice sounded distant and strange in his own ears. It was as if he were listening to a conversation on the other side of a thick wall. 'Let me see. I have to go in. I have to see what happened.'

'Now wait, boy, it's not pretty in there.'

But he knew he had to look. Deep inside he knew that whatever had happened to Vershan and his family must be linked to the raid on his own house. And that meant that it was his fault.

He pushed past the pulver and was standing in the doorway before anyone could stop him.

He looked in to the room. What he saw made him turn away again immediately. He bent double and threw up all over the pulver's boots.

Captured

The scene in Vershan's house was worse than anything he could have imagined. Vershan's father and mother were slumped against the wall in one corner. It looked as if they had been struck in the middle of their chests by an immense flame, for their upper bodies were charred and still smoking.

But even worse, lying on the floor next to an overturned chair he saw Vershan himself. Darion knew straight away that his friend was dead. His chest showed the same scorch marks as those on his parents' bodies. He saw the strange angle of Vershan's head, and knew that his neck had been broken.

Darion wiped his mouth. He tried to straighten up. 'S.. sorry,' he gasped as the pulver took a handkerchief from his pocket and began wiping his boots.

'Don't worry lad,' he said. 'Nasty, nasty thing. Wouldn't mind throwin' up meself.'

'Brannoch attack,' said the second pulver standing behind him. 'Couldn't be anything else.'

'Better check the other houses nearby,' said his colleague. 'See if any more children are missing like a couple of weeks ago.'

At first Darion thought they could be right. It might be another brannoch attack like the one yesterday. But what if it wasn't? What if it *was* linked to the stolen bottle from Tur's room?

He doubled up and was violently sick again. This time, the pulver had chance to step out of the way.

After he had finished emptying his stomach and his hacking coughs had stopped, Darion stood up. He stepped back towards the house, forcing himself to look into the room again, to search for clues.

He could feel Larena's hand grip his shoulder. He swallowed, feeling the filthy grime of vomit still in his throat.

'Don't go in, Darion, please don't.'

'Get off me!' he said. She recoiled from him as if he had slapped her.

'Sorry,' he said. 'I have to.'

'It's alright,' her fingers reached towards his arm again.

He swallowed hard once more and pulled away from Larena's touch. He turned and stepped into the room.

Behind him, one of the pulver guards called out. 'Boy! Come out of there. What are you doing?'

Darion just ignored him. He didn't even hear Larena's voice telling the pulver to 'Leave him for a moment, for pity's sake.'

There was his friend, in that horrible, twisted position. Then Darion noticed that the boy had died while turning around on the floor. His right arm was stretched out. He could see that Vershan had been reaching towards something.

Just beyond Vershan's outstretched hand, Darion saw a number of small pieces of blue and green glass. The colours were unmistakable. It was the remains of Vershan's essence jar. It looked as if it had been ground into tiny fragments by a heavy boot. His mind was racing now. That jar, so much like his own, and so similar to the stolen one still in his pouch, had been deliberately destroyed.

They *were* looking for it. They had searched for it here, in Vershan's house, and when they had discovered that Vershan's jar was not what they were looking for, that Vershan was not the one who had gone into Tur's rooms, they had smashed it to pieces. Then they had killed him anyway.

"What had he done?' Darion thought to himself. '*What was it about what he had seen that was worth killing for?'*

Darion dropped to his knees next to his friend's body.

'I'm sorry,' he whispered. 'I'm so sorry.'

He felt so numb that he couldn't even cry anymore. Somewhere deep inside he remembered something his dad had told him about being in shock after a battle. He realised that must be what was happening to him now.

The pulver knelt down and helped him to get up. The soldier was being kind and more gentle all of a sudden. That didn't matter now. Nothing mattered. He allowed himself to be led out of Vershan's house. He let Larena hug him because he knew she was doing it to comfort herself, as well as him, and he didn't want to make anyone feel any worse than they already did.

'We have to take him now miss.' He heard one of the pulver say. 'Gretton Tur will want to question him about what he knows.'

These words finally shook Darion out of his haze. Why would a regular pulver guard think of taking him to Tur? Were these really pulver soldiers? Guards of the city? Or could they be Gretton Tur's agents, deliberately sent to find him? If all of tonight's terrible events had happened because Tur was trying to find him and the stolen essence jar, Darion knew he would be murdered the moment Tur saw him. He had to get away from the pulver as quickly as he could.

They held him up between them as the three of them moved down the street. They would soon be on the edge of the city square close to the college buildings. From there it would take less than five minutes to reach Tur's private quarters.

Darion wracked his brains to think of how he could escape. The pulver were a lot stronger than he was. He could tell that from the grip on his arms. Both were probably much faster than him too. So, he couldn't fight them. He couldn't outrun them. He would have to trick them. Then perhaps he could lose himself in the crowds.

That was his only chance.

He started to think of everything he knew about the layout of the nearby streets. At the end of Vershan's quiet side alley was a busier road. They were nearly there. He glanced ahead and could make out the shapes of several people crisscrossing the main street in front of them.

They came out upon the first of two busy roads. After crossing them at this time of night, he knew that their route would take them back through dark side streets again. By then it would be too late. If he was going to make his escape, it had to be now.

Annoyingly, the two guards seemed to increase their grip on him as they pushed through the crowds. How could he get away? He stumbled between them. His boot stitching was flapping apart again. Of course! That was it! Suddenly he had an excuse to make them stop. But he had to choose exactly the right moment.

Less than fifty paces remained. Then they would have reached the quiet alleys – he would never get away if they went in there; there would be no more chance to escape. He ran through what he was about to say in his head. He knew what he was going to do. But which way would he go?

Forty paces left. Thirty.

The gloom of the alleys rose up before them. He felt excitement rise in his throat.

Twenty paces.

He had to do it now. But his voice wouldn't work. His throat had closed up with fear.

Ten paces. Five.

Finally he managed to let out a surprised cry. At the same moment he stumbled on his tattered boot.

'Ouch!' he cried out.

'Come on young man, pick up your feet will you?'

'Sorry, could we stop a moment?'

'What is it?' They still gripped his arms.

'Look.' He lifted his leg. The pulver saw the flapping patch of leather on his boot. 'I tripped. Can I just tie it up?'

'Huh, you need a new pair, lad.'

'I know, it's happened before. Sorry.'

As he said this he shrugged out of their grasp. He bent down between them and began to push the leather back into place.

'It'll only take a moment,' he said as he glanced around him. He saw three men walking towards them from the right. Turning to the other side he saw a young couple approaching in the other direction. They were laughing, arm in arm and walking with their heads bent close together.

'Hurry up,' the other pulver grumbled. 'We haven't got all night.'

'Nearly there.' Darion rapidly wound his knotty bootlace around the leather to stop it tripping him for real as soon as he ran.

The three men were right next to him now. The couple coming the other way started to move to one side to avoid the crush on the pavement.

Darion took his chance. He pushed himself up from his crouched position. Before the pulver guards could do anything, he sprinted away. His shoulder barged into the young couple as he ran, pushing them both into the pulver. The man gave a surprised cry.

'Sorry!' He yelled behind him.

'Get him,' yelled one of his guards. 'Stop that boy!'

But Darion had changed direction. Now he was already ducking between the three men, and running past them. They stopped in their tracks and turned to look after him. He couldn't help risking a look backwards as he ran. Just as he had hoped, the men were now getting in the way of the pulver as they started to chase him. He heard one of them call angrily; 'Out of our way, idiots. He'll get away!'

He increased his pace, adrenaline driving his legs faster than usual. His plan was to use the crowds in the streets to lose his pursuers, and then duck into an alleyway or sidestreet.

It was working so far. He found it was far easier for him to dodge between people than it was for the two adults chasing him. Already he had gained some distance. There were several people between them now and he knew that he could make it. For the first time he felt confident that he would escape.

He didn't count on the crowds also helping his pursuers though. With another cry of 'Stop him!' a burly man in brightly coloured fabrics grabbed at his arm as he swerved past. The man didn't quite manage to get a firm hold of him, but it was enough to make Darion stumble off balance. He fell into another man who did manage to hold onto him for several seconds. He squirmed and wriggled in the man's grip. He knew that the pulver would be gaining every second. 'Please sir, let me go.'

'Hold him,' yelled the burly man.

'Sir, I've done nothing wrong.'

They were nearer now.

'Stay still, lad,' said the man holding onto him.

'Please, sir, I haven't done anything.'

'Then we can sort it all out and there's nothing to worry over.'

'Sorry about this,' Darion replied and kicked the man in the shins.

His captor gave a loud yell of pain. 'Why you little brat…'

'Hold him!'

This time the pulver guard's voice was much nearer.

'Seer's blood, don't let him get away!'

'Did you see what that boy did? Damn near broke my leg.'

The man he had kicked had grabbed hold of one of the guards. The other slowed down to help his colleague.

'I want to make an official complaint.'

'Let go of me you fool!'

'We have to hurry sir.'

'You saw the brat. He attacked me.'

'And we'll never catch him if you don't…'

Darion realised that his plan had worked. It was too late for them to catch up with him now. He knew exactly where he was. Only a few paces away was a narrow cut-through that he and Vershan used as a short cut to get to the college buildings. There was a maze of side alleys and ginnels that he knew like the back of his hand. He had played dozens of games of 'hide-and-catch-up' here. Before the men behind him had finished arguing he had already squirreled his way through a gate and taken two turnings. After a few more seconds the angry shouts had faded. Not bothering to look behind him now, he sprinted along the backstreets into the very guts of Beltheron City.

Refuge at Fasker's

D arion jinked this way and that every time a new alley or ginnel opened up in front of him. It was really dark now; the gas lights of the main streets never filtered this far into the alleys. Even so he knew he wouldn't get lost. He looked up and could make out the shadow of a familiar balcony where he had scrambled up and hidden from Vershan during one of their games. It had only been a month ago. The memory brought an ache to his chest. For the first time it really hit home that Vershan was dead. Really dead, not pretend. Not like in a game. Now they would never play another game. They would never, *ever* share any more jokes. Thinking about this made him slow down. He started gasping for breath, and it was not just because of all the running.

Ahead was the back door of the candy merchant who used to take pity on the two of them when they were little. He could always be trusted to give them a free fistful of sweet-smelling treats from his store. Perhaps the old man would be of help again now, Darion thought. It was worth a try. He was badly out of breath by now and needed somewhere to rest up for a while. He raced towards the back door.

It seemed as if his luck was holding out. As he approached the back of the store, the door opened and the old candy merchant himself appeared. He bent down and released a furry shape onto the ground. His ancient pet cat was going out for the night.

'Good evening Mr Fasker sir,' Darion said.

Fasker straightened up and squinted into the dark alley. 'Who's that there?'

'Darion Melgardes, sir, remember? Vershan's friend.' Using Vershan's name out loud made his voice crack. He had to swallow hard. His throat was hurting.

The man's eyes grew wide. He smiled. 'Little Melgardes. Heh, heh! I haven't seen you and your greedy friend here for months. Not so little now I see.'

Darion couldn't find his voice. The kind words, the familiar face, the memories of his friend were all too much. He crumpled onto the ground at the man's feet and burst into tears.

*   *   *   *

Darion woke up in blackness. He was covered in a soft blanket. There was a pillow cushioning his head. He was warm. And comfortable. For a wonderful moment he thought that he was back at home, in his own room. He imagined that all of the horrors of the last few hours had been a terrible nightmare, nothing more. He almost expected his mother to pull back his curtains and call him for breakfast. In fact, he could smell it cooking. His nostrils twitched and he felt the saliva fill his mouth expecting food.

Darion stretched out. His eyes were beginning to adjust to the dark and he could make out vague shapes around the room. Unfamiliar shapes. This was not his room. His heart lurched and all thought of food left him. In an aching heartbeat he remembered it all. His mother being dragged from the house, the horror of Vershan's body, being chased by the pulver soldiers and finally being found by the old man.

He pulled the sheets closer around him. He didn't want to move, felt unable to get up. Darion just wanted to stay where he was forever. Perhaps eventually he would forget everything. As long as he stayed here, nothing else bad would happen.

He cursed himself under his breath as he realised that this was foolish. He was thinking like a child and had to grow up fast. Nothing would ever be the same again, and sooner or later, they would find him. For the hundredth time in the last twelve hours he told himself that it was too late to take the essence jar back, too late to say sorry. Vershan was dead and nothing could ever change that, never. Not only that, his mother had been taken away. For all he knew she could be dead by now as well, killed by those who questioned her as they tried to find out where he was.

Tears started to sting his eyes again and he gulped back a sob.

'No,' he said out loud. 'Stop feeling sorry for yourself. You've done too much crying already. That won't solve anything. You have to think, Darion. Think!'

Lying in the strange bed he tried to piece together all of the things that had happened. If he could figure out why he was being chased, what Tur's secret was and why it was so important, then maybe he could find a way to save himself and his mother... if she was even still alive.

He wracked his memory to think of anyone he could go to for help. He winced at the thought of putting anyone else in danger.

Harrow? Could he trust his teacher? Darion didn't feel confident enough to go to him. Matthien? Would his new friend still take his side when he discovered he had done such foolish things?

Alianna? The thought of having to confess to her about the mess he had got himself into was too much to bear.

As he was considering his options – there weren't very many, he had to admit – the old man coughed from behind the curtain.

'Young Darion, are you up?'

'Give me a moment.'

'No need to worry or hurry. But breakfast is ready.'

'Thanks, I'll be there in a minute.'

'I'll give you some light.'

Fasker parted the curtains. Early morning sunshine flooded into the room, along with a stronger scent of cooking breakfast. Mushrooms and eggs, he guessed.

Darion threw back his bed covers. He had slept fully dressed and his clothes were twisted and tangled. His eyes were dazzled by the morning light after such thick blackness. He scrabbled around by the bed until his found his boots.

Really hungry now he pulled them on and stepped into the main room behind Fasker's shop.

It was filled with a busy collection of everything from cooking utensils to shovels and spades. There were books and documents lining the shelves, and candles, and bottles and jars of sweets everywhere. It was obviously where Fasker spent most of his time, and did most of his work.

Soon Darion was tucking into the breakfast greedily. He lifted a hunk of bread to his mouth. It was spread thickly with salty butter and soaked with the bright yellow egg yolk from his plate. Tearing at it with his teeth, he wolfed it down. The yolk ran down his chin, but he didn't care. He thought it was the most delicious thing he had ever tasted.

When had he last eaten? It must have been twenty hours ago at least.

'Slow down a little lad,' his host grinned.

Darion gulped heavily. 'Sorry sir.'

'I don't mind your manners, but you'll choke yourself if you're not careful. Take your time. The food's not going anywhere.'

He nodded and took another gulp.

'Here's something to wash it down.'

He placed a steaming mug next to Darion's plate.

'When you're ready, perhaps you can tell me what led you to my door last night?'

This did make him slow down. How much could he tell this old man who had helped him so much? Dare he tell him anything at all? Too many people had already suffered because of him. He dreaded putting anyone else in danger.

'I'm old,' the candy merchant said. 'But I'm no fool. That's one thing that you young ones always get wrong. You think that once a person has more grey and white in their hair than black or brown, their wits must be jelly.' He narrowed his eyes at Darion, but they were still soft and friendly. 'Well it's not so my young friend, not so,' he said. He tapped at his temples, where his hair was *very* white. 'I still know a thing or two up here and I still have the use of my eyes and ears. I can recognise pulver soldiers as much now as when I was a lad, and it's not hard to guess at their anger when they shout at each other the way they did in the streets last night.'

'What did you hear?' Darion asked.

'Not much. Well not all that much that made sense. But enough to guess they had lost something important.'

Darion stopped chewing.

'Something, or some*one*,' the old man continued.

Darion looked away. He stared into the corner, as if the pile of boots lying there was suddenly very interesting.

'Now don't you go fretting and worrying. Just because they work for the High Lord and his Guild doesn't mean the pulver are always right. Or even *in* the right.' He paused a moment, looking at Darion, giving him time to speak. 'Does it, my lad?'

Darion shook his head slowly. 'No sir it doesn't.'

'You and your young friend might have a taste for a few free candies every now and then, but I think I'm a good enough judge of a boy's character to say that you aren't such a bad one, eh? Not a real thief?'

The boy shook his head again.

'I'm not sir. Honest I'm not.'

'And what could a young lad like you have done to be worth the rage of a whole bunch of them anyway, eh? For a long time I've said that the pulver are given too much power in our streets. Arrests, beatings, and worse my lad. Oh yes, I've seen them do terrible things in my time. Been on the wrong end of a pulver stick myself on occasion - and for no good reason either.'

'Like what?' It felt odd but Darion was desperate to know. After all he had seen, somehow the idea that this old man had also been through horrors and survived them, was a comfort to Darion.

The old man stared at him. He settled down into his chair and sipped at his steaming mug of coffee.

'You want another drink?'

Darion nodded. He pushed his own mug across the table. His host started to pour the strong black liquid from the pot.

'It's got a whole lot worse recently,' he began. 'The pulver used to be men you went to if you were in trouble, bothered by noisy neighbours, a victim of break-ins, or violence in the streets.' He looked away and stared into the corner of the room, his thoughts far away. 'But in the last few months, well, it's almost as if they're not the same men. They ignore a plea for help as often as not. I know an old woman called Mater Jenka. She's a grandmother to three lovely young things. She lives a few streets away in the Cittegarre. Well, there was a silkefox and its mate worrying at old Mater Jenka's doors, looking for food. You wouldn't believe how brave these silkefoxes have become. Mater Jenka tried to shoo them away but it was no good. So she sent for the evening pulver guard to scare them off. That's all, just to scare them. One would have been enough, but five guards turned up. Five! Usually they bang a couple of sticks together, make a big shape by waving their arms and it's enough. But they had swords and bows, whole quivers full of arrows. As if they were going on a hunt.'

'It's illegal to kill the foxes,' Darion said.

'And rightly so. I think it's a sin to kill a creature just for the sake of it. Oh, I know those silkefoxes can be a nuisance, but no real danger unless they're threatened. No, the idea is - the *law* is - to scare them away from the city. Well it was obvious straightaway what these pulver meant to do. They shot at the poor beasts. The female was killed straightaway and they bundled her into a sack. Carried her away for the seer only knows what.'

'They took the body?'

'It hardly had time to fall to the ground before it was carted off. The male was winged by an arrow, but it ran into the shadows.'

'What did the pulver do then?' A strange memory was bothering Darion. Something that had been said to him recently. Or was it something he had seen? He knew it had been about the silkefoxes, or the pedjiaar. What was it? He tried to remember, but the thought kept swirling away like morning fog on a river.

'Well they chased it down,' the old man was saying. 'Determined they were. More than just determined. They were *desperate* to get it. At least that's what I'd say.'

'But that doesn't make sense,' Darion said. 'It couldn't do any more harm if it was injured. Silkefoxes just slink off if they're hurt or feel threatened.'

'Course they do lad, course they do. That's what I mean, there was no *need* to do it. No need at all, just a meanness. T*hat's* what's crept into this city lad, meanness, and I'm telling you it's far more dangerous than even a hunting pedjiaar.' He nodded to himself. 'A meanness in this world, and it's in men's hearts.'

He took another gulp from his coffee.

'So I trust you lad, that's what I'm saying,' he went on. 'I believe that you didn't do anything wrong. The pulver, the mages, even the High Lord himself are over-reacting to everything these days. You might just have accidentally kicked over a bucket, or disturbed their guard dog's sleep and they'd still come after you like you had plotted treachery and rebellion itself.'

This made Darion run through the possibilities once more. Was he mistaken about things after all? Could it all be just some ghastly coincidence? Were the pulver just over-reacting, like Fasker said?

Was there a chance that his mother had been arrested for some other reason? Stealing perhaps. He knew how desperate they were for money, how hard it had been lately to put food on the table. If she had been tempted to take some bread from a market stall, or leave a merchant without paying, might they have come looking for her for that?

And Vershan? The name still stabbed at his heart like a draccen claw. It was just possible the tragedy that had happened to Vershan's family was unconnected. Had one of the pedjiaar roaming near the city walls attacked? Had one of them grown so hungry that it had got into Vershan's home and...? Darion shivered at the thought and tried to push the image out of his head.

No. He knew that he was just fooling himself. He dismissed all of these ideas as being impossible. They were all just excuses to make himself feel better. He knew his mother carried the same pride, and held the same ideals that his father had. She would starve before steal. And the horrors that he had seen in Vershan's house, the scorch marks, the twisted neck, those were not the signs of a pedjiaar attack.

No. No matter how much he tried to distance himself from all that had happened Darion knew that it all came back to him. There were just too many incidents, too many coincidences all on that one night.

He took Tur's essence jar out of his bag. Turning it over in his fingers he spoke softly to himself. 'You've caused too much trouble, I should just throw you away.'

But of course it wasn't the jar itself. The jar was only important because it proved he had been in Tur's room. They were terrified about what he might have seen while he was there. Again he remembered the look of fear in the old mage's eyes as he stepped behind the curtain, and the strange sounds he had heard coming from the chamber beyond. What had Tur being doing to the pedjiaar on the table?

The pedjiaar. The silkefoxes around the city. We're they all connected?

If they were, then the connection was secret enough – and serious enough - for Tur's men to want to kill him.

And, he reasoned, those hunting him wouldn't have taken any chances. That's why they arrested his mother too. Just in case he had told her. And everyone knew that he shared all his secrets with Vershan. Anyone that Tur's men asked would have told them that Vershan was the first person that Darion would have gone to to tell him what he had seen. The thought hit him again like a punch in the stomach. His friend had been killed just to keep him quiet. And he hadn't even known anything.

So Darion knew without a doubt, if they had murdered Vershan *just in case*, they were certain to do the same to him as soon as they caught him.

He shuddered at the thought of poor Vershan's twisted neck. The viciousness had shocked him to his bones. The idea of such cruelty turned like a vileworm in his guts.

'There was no need,' he said to himself. 'No need.'

He wiped a tear from his eye but he couldn't stop more from coming. They ran down his face until his cheeks were soaked and his nose ran.

'Snot for cobwebs,' he remembered.

*   *   *   *

It was later that evening. Darion had rested up during the day with Fasker, the candy merchant, before beginning to fall asleep in his chair. The old man had bundled him up to his room, to rest properly. Darion was in the middle of a dream where Alianna was asking him who had told the pulver that it was *his* broken jar on Tur's shelf. He was struggling to find an answer for her. It seemed important that he should know this, but before he could work it out he felt a hand shaking his shoulder. The thought faded.

'Come on my lad, wake up. Time to go.' The candy merchant's voice held a note of panic.

Darion leapt up on the bed.

'Jorian! It must have been Jorian who told them...' he shouted.

'Hush!' The old man held a hand over Darion's mouth. He jumped back. Then the boy heard heavy footsteps and voices outside.

'I'm afraid they've found you boy. Follow me.'

Darion did as he was told and they crossed behind a curtain at the rear of the storeroom. For a second, it reminded Darion of the tapestry covering the entrance to Tur's secret room and he shivered.

There was an old door beyond, low down, cut into the brickwork.

'Through here,' hissed the candy merchant. 'And I hope you're not afraid of small spaces.'

Darion pushed his way through the tight entrance. He had to bend double to fit through. The corridor inside was even worse. He crouched low, but still his back scraped against the rough stones of the roof. Fasker wasn't much bigger than him, but even so he was almost forced onto his hands and knees to squeeze along behind. Feeling in front of him with both feet and fingers Darion inched forwards. More than once he knocked his head sharply on a jutting rock, and tripped over the uneven ground. But he couldn't stop. Fasker's hand was always at his back, pushing him on.

The air in the tunnel was damp and stale. Darion was soon gasping to get a clear breath into his lungs. It smelt of decay and old rotten food - like when he had to take out the rubbish from the kitchen for the Beltheron street cleaners to dispose of.

It was dark in front of him but flickers of light and shadow were thrown forwards by the torch stick the candy seller was holding. Darion saw the shadow of his own profile cast up on the wall, distorted and constantly changing.

On and on they went. He was stumbling more often now, even though his eyes had grown more accustomed to the gloomy surroundings. He was exhausted and doubted he could go on much longer. Darion thought that they must have walked for at least an hour already. Whereabouts under the city could they be?

'A bit further boy, not long now,' said the candy merchant. It was as if he had read his mind.

Sure enough, after a few more minutes of gasping and shuffling the floor started to rise upwards. It got steeper for several paces until Darion was forced onto all fours, scrabbling with both hands and feet to climb. It began to get darker too. The light from the torch stick behind him had been growing dimmer for some time.

'Almost there,' said his old guide. 'And just in time, my light is spent.'

As he said these words, the torch stick did in fact sputter out and Darion had to feel his way in total blackness over the last few metres.

'Ouch!' He struck his head against something hard and solid.

'We're there at last,' Fasker said. 'Just give a knock will you?'

Darion reached in front of him and felt a heavy wooden door blocking his way. He made a fist with his right hand and rapped sharply.

'That's it my boy. Don't worry my young friend, we won't have long to wait.'

Darion could already hear a faint, distant movement somewhere on the other side of the door.

There was the clanking of a key being turned, the creak of rusting door hinges and a sudden flood of light. Darion pitched forwards onto a green and grey carpet.

He rolled over and looked up. Standing over him, wearing a patched dressing gown and furry slippers, was his essencing master, Cleve Harrow.

Harrow Reveals More Secrets

Darion, Cleve Harrow and Fasker were sitting around Harrow's dining table. Harrow had brewed a pot of strong tea. He poured some out for each of them. Darion warmed his hands around his cup.

'Start at the beginning, Fasker,' said Harrow. 'When exactly did you find the boy?'

'It was late last night,' Fasker replied. 'After the ten bell certainly. Perhaps even later.'

He began to tell Harrow about all that had happened. Darion occasionally interrupted, adding a detail to his story, or something he had forgotten to mention to the old man earlier.

Harrow's eyes remained fixed on Darion throughout. *As if he's trying to look into my mind,* Darion thought. *'Can mages do that?'* he wondered.

At last, between them, they reached the end of their tale.

Harrow carried on looking at Darion in silence for several moments. When he did finally say something, his voice was like the rusty scrape of a knife.

'And you brought him here? What were you thinking?' He turned away and raised a hand to rub at his eyes. His shoulders rose, then sank again as he gave a sigh.

'This is bad,' he murmured to himself. 'This is one of the first places they'll think of. I'm surprised they're not here already.'

He got to his feet and hurried to the window. He glanced up and down the street then dropped the shutters.

There was something frightening in Harrow's reaction to his story, Darion thought. Harrow usually knew exactly what to do. Even when the brannoch attacked the classroom, Harrow had stayed calm. It was as though nothing could shake him. Now though, Darion realised that his teacher was terrified.

Cleve Harrow passed his hand over his face again. 'We probably don't have long,' he said. 'Darion my boy, I'm afraid that the people who are looking for you will soon come here. They will suspect I am hiding you.'

'But, but why would they think that?' asked Darion. 'There's no reason I would think of coming here. I didn't even know where you lived.' He paused for a moment. 'I still don't know, come to think of it. I lost all track of where I was down in Fasker's tunnels.'

'And has it not occurred to you to ask exactly *why* Fasker has a tunnel leading straight to my cellar door?'

Darion looked blankly at him. He shot a glance back across to Fasker. The old candy merchant didn't seem to want to catch his eyes. He looked down into a far corner of the room. 'It hadn't, no, but now you come to mention it...' he remembered what the Cleve had told the class about being an ament. 'Is an ament another word for a sp..."

'Not a word!' Fasker interrupted. 'Not here, not now.'

He was looking around anxiously, as if he didn't even trust Harrow's walls not to be listening in to their conversation.

'We are safe,' said Harrow. 'From being overheard at least. However we don't have much time.' He began to rummage around in a leather satchel hung over the back of a chair.

'Yes Darion, the word ament doesn't just mean one who knows magic. It also refers to spies, those who work as agents using magic for secret purposes.

'You still have a lot to learn, my boy,' said Harrow. 'Things that you don't understand.'

In spite of his words a few moments ago, Harrow now dropped his voice to a whisper. Darion had to lean in closely to hear what he said.

'What did you take from Tur's rooms?'

The question rocked Darion back on his heels. Harrow knew!

'Quickly, boy. What did you take?'

'I...I...'

'Come on, it must have been something important.'

Finally Darion slumped down into a chair. He was going to have to own up.

'I'm sorry Harrow, sir, I didn't mean for anything like this to happen. I never thought I was doing anything so wrong.'

'Enough. Time for apologies later, what was it that it is so important for Tur and the High Lord's men to chase you halfway across the city?'

The High Lord's men? Jorian's father was chasing him? Then he remembered the conversation at the party about Tur and Lord Argolin being involved together. Things were getting worse.

'Just a jar, an essence jar,' Darion blurted out. He had no choice. He knew that he had to tell everything. He felt a sense of relief as he started to speak.

'A few days ago,' he began. 'The day before the brannoch attack, I went out searching for feathers.'

'The homework I set you?'

Darion nodded. 'I chased a green sparrow into the bushes, got stuck, tripped and dropped my essence jar.'

'It broke?'

'Smashed to pieces. I daren't tell anyone. You, my mother... definitely not my mother. I tried to mend it but it still didn't look right. I was scared.'

'So when I sent you on your little errand to Gretton Tur's rooms...' Harrow let the rest of the sentence hang in the air.

Darion nodded. Now he had started to explain, it was beginning to feel easier. 'I went in on my own. Tur was busy, on his way out. I didn't plan to do it, in fact I...I... oh I wish I'd never started any of this!'

'It is too late to feel sorry about that now,' said Harrow. 'The damage is done. It was a foolish mistake, but whatever has happened since then is *not* your fault. Do you understand me?'

Darion was silent. He wasn't sure if Harrow was right when he said that things weren't his fault. Guilt still gnawed at him like a rat nibbling a sack of food scraps.

'But *what* is so important about that jar?' said Harrrow.

'Sir, it's not that sir. Or at least, I don't think it is.'

Harrow looked at him.

'What do you mean?'

'It's not because I took the jar that they want to catch me. It's what they think I discovered.'

'Go on.'

'While I was there, in Tur's room, I saw something. Something in another room. Tur was doing something to a...to a...well, it looked like a pedjiaar, from what I could see of it.'

'A pedjiaar?'

Fasker and Harrow looked at each other sharply.

'Yes sir, Tur had it tied down to a table and he had a syringe in his hand. A bit like the ones we use in class.'

Harrow was leaning forwards now, his face only inches from Darion's.

'And what next? Hurry, Darion tell me. What did Tur do?'

'I think...well sir, I think he injected the pedjiaar with something. It obviously hurt it sir, not like when we use an animal in class for something. This one was frightened sir. It was in pain.'

'Did you see anything else? What happened after he injected the poor creature?'

'I'm afraid I don't know sir. I was too scared to stay any longer. I just wanted to get out.'

Harrow was silent, deep in thought.

'It's what we suspected isn't it?' said Fasker.

'Yes, it would seem so,' Harrow replied.

'What?' Darion said. 'What was he doing? Harrow? Mr Fasker? What was Tur doing to the pedjiaar?'

But Harrow wasn't listening any more. He had crossed to the shelves that lined the far side of his study. It was Fasker who answered his question.

'It would have been something wicked and secret whatever it was. Tur is only interested in wickedness.'

'So I'm right,' said Darion. 'He *is* frightened about me telling anyone what I saw.' He paused a moment before carrying on. 'There's something else too, something I overheard at a party in the Variegatt.'

Harrow raised his eyes. The thought of young Melgardes at a Variegatt party was surprising to say the least.

'What did you hear? The best you can remember it.'

'The Maraglar merchants were talking,' Darion began. 'Something about Tur and Argolin taking power. How Lord Arteris wouldn't be in control much longer and something else about Tur being close to success, and, and,' he struggled to remember the final words he had heard, before Jorian had dragged him away behind the curtain. 'Something about getting to the midst? *In* the midst of something? And one of Lord Matthien's friends, Halperth, he talked about Argolin taking control as well. But I don't know what it means. I wish I'd never gone into that room. I've told you everything, but I still don't understand.

And now, because of me they've taken my mother. And Vershan is…is…'

Harrow laid a calming hand on his arm. 'You had no way of knowing that what you did – crazed, irresponsible as it might have been – could have led to such disaster.' Harrow sighed. He thought for several seconds. 'Midst. *Midst*? Mix?' His eyes sparkled with an idea. 'Is it possible that the word was mixture?' he asked.

Darion immediately realised what his teacher meant. 'Of course,' he said. 'That would make sense. They must have been talking about creating a mixture for an experiment. And that's what I saw in Tur's rooms! An experiment he was doing with the pedjiaar. Is that what you think?'

Harrow nodded. 'Yes Darion, that is exactly what I think. You have been caught up in events far bigger than you could imagine,' he said. 'We have suspected for some time that Gretton Tur is conducting his own experiments using essencing techniques.' He looked at Fasker. 'As you said a moment ago my old friend, we have known all along that his motives are evil.'

'Aye, his reasons are all selfish and cruel.'

'And from what you have just told me Darion, it is easy to guess that he and Argolin are working together – quite possibly to take over Beltheron City itself.

'We cannot change what happened last night. What's done is done. It is too late to worry about wishing things were different.' Harrow raised his arm towards the table in the corner. 'Fasker, bring me that bottle over there.'

Fasker hurried to get it.

'This one?'

'Yes,' Harrow clicked his fingers impatiently. 'Give it to me. Quickly.'

He picked it up and handed it to the Cleve.

'Now, keep an eye on the street.'

The old candy merchant nodded and went to the window. He looked through, glancing up and down the dark road outside.

'We cannot change what has already happened,' Harrow said again. 'But we might be able to stop things getting worse. The first step is to get you out of here. To a place of real safety. Darion?'

'Yes sir?'

'I hope you're not scared of heights.'

'*First small spaces and now heights,*' Darion thought to himself. '*What next?*'

'Heights?' he repeated. 'Why, what do you mean? What are you going to do?'

'Now, Darion my boy,' Harrow said in a friendlier tone. 'Do you remember your father?'

This seemed such a strange question in the circumstances, but Darion didn't have time to think about it. He nodded.

'Yes of course I remember him.'

'Then you will remember that he was a courageous man.'

Darion nodded again.

'He was even more brave than you know,' Harrow continued. His voice had dropped to an even quieter whisper. 'Now is not the time to explain, but your father and I worked together. He was a hero, Darion. You hear me? A hero.'

The thought that Cleve Harrow had worked with his father made Darion's head spin.

'I need you to be like him,' Harrow went on. 'You must be very brave now Darion.'

Darion's eyes were like saucers as he stared at his teacher. 'Was he... was he...?'

Harrow nodded. 'He was a spy. And he was a master of essencing, Darion. An ament, like me.'

While he had been speaking, Harrow had taken the stopper from the bottle that Fasker had just given him.

'Your father worked with me, and now, so does your n..'

But before Harrow could say another word, Fasker spun around from his viewpoint at the window.

'Harrow,' he said. 'We have visitors.'

The Cleve turned and sped to the curtains. He glanced through them quickly and pulled them closed.

'They are coming. Three of them.'

'Three what?' Darion asked.

Harrow didn't reply. He just barked another order at Fasker. 'Check the alley.' He pointed through a doorway that led to a small back room. 'The window through there. Go!'

Fasker moved silently into the other room. Darion's heart squeezed with tension. He tried to swallow but it was as though a hand had clenched around his throat.

Fasker came back in a couple of moments. His face was grim.

'Four more that way, coming fast,' he said. 'And another two waiting on the other corner of the street.'

'Both of you, upstairs,' said Harrow. 'Now!'

They ran to the staircase. Harrow grabbed two more jars and a long, narrow box from his desk as he hurried past.

Darion had just reached the bottom step when he heard a hard, rapid knock on the door. He stopped and looked around. Fasker almost bumped into him.

Harrow waved them both upstairs with an urgent, angry gesture.

'Who's there?' he called out.

'Gretton Tur's men of the guard,' came the reply from outside.

'Tur's men you say? What on earth can you want at this late hour?'

'We are on orders from Tur and Lord Argolin himself,' came the official voice. 'You must open this door.'

Darion could still hear the voices as he crept up the steps. Fasker's hand was on the small of his back, pushing him on.

'Give me a moment, friend,' Harrow called through the door. 'I have the key here somewhere. Let me look.'

As he finished speaking, Harrow followed them upstairs.

The three of them entered the Cleve's small sleeping room at the top of the house. There was another louder knock from below.

'Harrow,' the voice outside was getting more impatient. 'Find the key quickly or you'll have to find a new door too. This one will be broken down.'

'Be with you in a moment,' Harrow yelled down. 'It's here somewhere.'

He placed the vial, jars and other objects on the bed.

'Darion, come here.'

Darion stepped towards him. he could see a couple of centimetres of thick, yellow liquid in the bottom of the vial.

'Fasker,' Harrow instructed. 'Open the skylight.'

'Cleve, what are you going to do?' Darion's voice sounded thin and reedy in his own ears, betraying how frightened he was.

'I'm extending your essencing studies my boy,' he smiled grimly. 'Consider this a bit of extra homework.'

'But...'

Another heavier knocking came from the door below.

'No time to argue! Remember I asked you about heights?'

Darion nodded. 'I don't *think* I'm scared of them sir.'

'Now's the time to find out.'

Harrow picked a black feather from the narrow box he had brought upstairs with him. He plunged the feather into the vial of liquid and shook it violently. From another of the bottles he added a few drops of grey smoky fluid. Darion recognised it as the transforming mutabar liquid they used in class. He gulped. He knew what was coming next.

'You know that this will not allow you to actually fly,' Harrow explained quickly. 'The essencing will not actually turn you into a bird. But it will allow you to *leap* most effectively. Certainly enough for you to escape our pursuers over the rooftops.'

Darion nodded. He couldn't speak. He was too nervous, too excited…too frightened.

'We'll keep them as busy as we can to give you the best chance. Fasker, keep an eye on them.' He handed Fasker the final bottle from the bed. 'If they break in, throw this down the steps at them. That should put them off for a while.' Picking up the essencing mixture he had just been preparing, he pushed the vial towards Darion.

'Drink this down,' he ordered.

Darion hesitated. What would happen? What would it feel like?

'Drink it down! All of it! Now!'

Then a heavy crash from downstairs stopped all thought. He snatched at the vial and gulped at the liquid inside.

'Out of the window, quickly!' his teacher hissed.

Harrow pushed him towards the skylight window. Fasker ran to the top of the stairs. They could hear footsteps climbing the steps and more angry voices.

'Harrow! Are you up there?'

'Come out old man.'

'Where's the boy, Harrow? What have you done with him?'

Harrow was still pushing him out of the skylight. Fasker threw the botttle down at the voices.

There was no sound, but Darion was aware of a bright flash of green light behind him as he struggled out onto the rooftop tiles.

Sounds of coughing and even more furious shouts filled the house below. He tried to keep his balance on the slanting surface.

Then the effects of Harrow's potion hit him. Hard.

At first it was like a kick in his ribcage. His heart seemed to grow in his chest like a balloon. He gulped, but couldn't get his breath. Then a slimy feeling ran through his stomach and he thought he would be sick. He staggered backwards and almost tumbled back down through the window.

Harrow's hand was there to steady him.

'Go to the forest caves,' the Cleve whispered at him. 'Get out of the city.'

'Harrow, I'm going to be si...'

'No you're not! You won't be sick. The feeling will pass in a moment. Remember. The forest caves. I will find you.'

Darion shook his head to try to clear the pain. A sick feeling still clutched at his guts. But then, everything changed. The sickness and breathlessness suddenly felt like sunshine-filled sky after a thunderstorm. He felt powerful, energised.

Darion pushed up with his knees and felt himself soar away from the narrow opening of the skylight. Landing awkwardly on the steep rooftiles, he just about managed to steady himself. He threw out his arms to get a better balance. As he did it felt as if all the weight were taken from his legs. He felt no pressure on his feet. Darion looked down and saw that his toes were only just lightly touching the rooftop. Without thinking he adjusted the spread of his arms slightly and found himself perfectly at ease on the slippery, tilted surface. It was as if he was weightless. He dropped his arms to his sides again and immediately lost his balance as his full weight returned to his legs. Automatically his arms shot up again, twitching in the air. He felt the weightless feeling return.

Darion looked around to see how far he had jumped. To his amazement the leap had carried him out of the window and across most of the roof. He saw that he was already on the edge of the guttering. That was over four metres!

He had made hardly any effort. Was this what being a bird was like? How long would it last, he wondered?

There was another flash from inside the house. Smoke billowed through the open skylight behind him. Then more shouts, cursing, and Harrow's voice rising above it all with some deathly threat or incantation.

Darion heard one of the soldiers scream and then a thump as if something had collided heavily with the wall. He grinned as he remembered the Cleve 'hurling' Vershan across the classroom. He refocused his mind on escape. Turning back he gauged the distance to the guttering of the roof on the opposite side of the street. The road below was a wide one and he guessed that there were at least five metres of open air between them. He had just made a jump of over four metres without even trying, but could he manage such a huge leap as this? He peeped over the edge and the cobbles of the street far below yawned up at him making his stomach turn.

A further yell from behind him made his decision for him. With a deep breath he spread his arms wide, bent his knees and jumped.

Rooftops

For a long moment he felt himself climbing into the air. Wind whistled in his ears. He windmilled his arms wildly, but this twisted his whole body backward and brought his feet and legs up over his head. Gasping in panic he felt himself start to plunge towards the cobbles far below him.

But then, the essence of the bird took over. The borrowed instinct forced his arms into a wide, curved arc. He was just in time to catch a breath of wind. It lifted him back up to the level of the rooftops. Another slight adjustment of his fingers and he was soaring again. Thankfully he saw that he was gliding in the right direction. He was almost halfway to the next rooftop. With a couple more flaps of his arms he saw the gutter approach. He was still level with it, but was now losing height again. Like an exhausted swimmer reaching the edge of a pool he scrabbled frantically to grab a safe support.

This just tipped him forwards and down again. He wasn't going to make it! With one more desperate lurch he spread out his arms and legs in a wide X shape. His descent slowed down but he knew he was still too low. The gutter shot past just above him and he saw the rough bricks of the wall about to hit his face. Darion had once watched the red hawks skydancing over the city walls. He saw how they had switched direction and turned so easily. The memory shot through his whole being as he dropped one arm to his side. This movement twisted him in the air. The other arm scrabbled at the gutter and his fingers made contact! He slammed against the wall. The shock almost forced his fingers open again but somehow he managed to hold on. He hung under the guttering, swaying backwards and forwards.

Darion didn't know how long he could hold on. He felt the bird's essence leaving him. His shoulders were already numb with the effort, and his arms ached like never before. Then he heard a dreadful creaking groan. The end of the gutter that he was holding onto suddenly lurched away from the wall. It couldn't hold his weight! The groaning noise was following by cracking and splintering sounds. Darion looked up and saw one of the bolts that held the guttering twist out of the bricks. He felt himself swing away from the wall as more of the guttering came away from its fastenings. As it twisted, the freezing dirty rainwater gathered in the bottom of the gutter poured over him. He spluttered as some of it went into his mouth, but still he held on. The old metal was under tremendous pressure. If it cracked and split, he would drop down to the hard street below. '*How far was it to fall?*' he wondered to himself.

Legs swinging wildly beneath him, he tried to keep his grip. With another lurch, the gutter dropped further.

Luck was finally on his side. Rather than just cracking and breaking away, the gutter tilted and bent downwards. It was lowering him to the ground. If only he could hold on a few more seconds, perhaps he would be close enough to jump down to safety. Darion looked down between his arms, muscles and sinews screaming in agony. They felt heavier again, and clumsy, not like the graceful feeling of flight they had given him a few moments ago. It was no good, he was still too high up. But the length of guttering had now swung out so far that he was over halfway across the width of the street below him. With another jump and flap of his arms he thought could just about make it to the lower roof opposite. Steeling his nerve and gathering all of his remaining energy, he twisted and jumped sideways, flapping his exhausted arms as he went.

He landed heavily and rolled forwards. *'This will take a bit more practice,'* he thought.

But at least he had made it onto the lower roof. He glanced back and couldn't believe the distance he had already travelled. There was little chance of his pursuers finding him now.

'Just as well,' he thought. He could sense another change beginning in his arms. They were feeling even heavier. The essencing wasn't going to last much longer. He knew that he had to get down to street level quickly before all of the bird's abilities left him.

Spreading his arms one last time, he jumped down from the low roof. He fell slowly at first, but in the final moments felt the last of the power drain away from him. He dropped the last metre like a stone.

The ground hit him hard. Luckily he remembered to bend his knees on impact and he rolled over to cushion the blow. Even so he was badly winded and lay on the ground gasping to get his breath back.

Darion shuffled backwards towards the shelter of the wall. He huddled in the shadows, listening for anyone approaching. He had made quite a noise as he landed and didn't want anyone coming out of their home to investigate. After all he had gone through, he didn't want to be discovered and arrested again as a suspected night-thief!

Luckily no one seemed to have been disturbed. Darion stayed where he was for several minutes, exhausted, alone, and thoroughly miserable.

Strange Reunion

At long last, Darion dragged himself back onto his feet. The feeling in his arms was not so bad now, and he flexed his shoulders and fingers, testing for injury. There were no sharp stabs of pain, nothing that indicated he had injured himself. The gutter's stagnant water soaked his shirt. He shivered. Looking up and down the alley where he had been hiding, making sure once more he had not been seen, he set off and broke into a trot.

He picked up speed. He glanced behind him once more as he ran around the corner.

'Hey! Watch out!' Too late. Not looking where he was going, he crashed into someone coming the other way. The impact was so hard that both of them were knocked off their feet. They ended in a tangled mess on the ground.

'Clumsy fool,' the voice was familiar.

He caught a waft of perfume. He recognised it instantly. Honeysuckle and spices. He looked at the person he had collided with.

'Alianna!'

'Darion? What on earth?'

'I'm so sorry, are you alright?'

He struggled to get to his own feet so that he could help her as quickly as he could. In a moment they were both standing again.

'I'm fine,' Alianna said. 'But what's going on?'

As usual the sight of Alianna made his tongue stick to the roof of his mouth. He felt his face growing red. Why did he feel this way whenever she turned up?

'Not out essence hunting again?' she teased.

He forced a smile. He guessed it didn't look like a very good one.

'No. Not this time. No.'

She started to brush some mud off her trousers where she had fallen.

'Oh, gods, I'm so sorry...'

'No matter.' She smiled at him. Unlike his, *her* smile did look good.

'It's a pity you had to dash off from the party the other evening.' She seemed in a hurry to change the subject. 'The games were great fun just after you left. You really missed something.'

'Sorry. I should have said goodbye I...'

'Stop apologising. It's alright. Jorian said that you had to leave in a hurry.'

'I bet he did,' he thought to himself. *'I bet he couldn't wait to tell you.'*

'No matter anyway.' She frowned at him. 'You still haven't told me what happened to you, Darion. Look at you. You're filthy. And soaked!'

He looked down and saw the tattered state of his clothes. It was hardly surprising after the crawl through the underground tunnels with Fasker, and crashing to the ground just now, covered in filthy gutter water.

He must have looked like a scavenging rat. No wonder she looked so worried.

In fact, he noticed that she wasn't just worried about *him*. Now she started to glance nervously all around her. It was obvious she was frightened of something else as well.

'Were you being chased?' she said.

He didn't know what to say. He couldn't tell her that yes, he was being chased by pulver sent to look for him by none other than Jorian's father. How would he explain that, in the eyes of her friends, he was no more than a common thief. If he told her any of that she would think he was just a Tenementerra wretch. He'd never see her again.

Even so, he would have to tell her *something*.

'It's alright,' he said. 'You're right, I was being chased. By…by… By some boys in our street.' The lie came easily to him. 'But it's alright now. I got away.'

She looked at him strangely. 'Boys?'

He nodded.

'Look, Darion,' she said. 'If there's something really wrong, you can tell me.'

'No, its fine. Thanks… thank you.'

'Come on, you look shaken to bits.' Her hand reached out and before Darion knew what was happening she had taken his hand in hers. 'You're freezing too.' She felt his sleeve. 'And wet. Really Darion, what *have* you been doing? You need to get warm. I bet you haven't even had supper, have you?'

He shook his head, not able to look at her face.

'Come with me, let's get you cleaned up.'

Still holding onto his hand she began leading him down the street.

'Where are we going?' he asked her. Cleve Harrow had told him to get out of the city. He had to make his way to the forest caves. If Alianna insisted on taking him somewhere, he would be delayed. Worse still, he might be spotted by one of the pulver looking for him.

He tried to pull away from her. 'It's very kind Alianna, but I really must…'

'Don't be stupid. You're shivering. And hurt. I want to help.'

She was so insistent. Still looking around, her eyes darting from corner to corner of the street, she pulled him after her again.

'Alianna, I...' He froze. Coming around the corner were two pulver guards.

Alianna had seen them as well. Before he could think about what to do she dragged him into a doorway.

They both pressed back into the shadows. Darion could hear the voices of the pulver as they approached.

'He'll be far away by now. Must have climbed like a cat to get over those rooftops.'

'Gods save him if he *is* caught. If Argolin gets his hands on him and that old mage Harrow they'll never see the light of day again.'

'And I'm not looking forward to what he'll do to us when we tell him they got away.'

Darion listened intently as they got closer. So, they hadn't caught Harrow. He and Fasker must have escaped.

The voices continued.

'Well let's keep looking then.'

'We've the lords' only chance of finding him now.'

'If I see him again I'll...'

They were past them now, turning the corner. Darion realised he hadn't even breathed the whole time. Alianna pressed tight into him as they pushed themselves as far back in the doorway as they could.

She moved her finger up to his lips, telling him to keep quiet.

Several more moments passed. Finally her shoulders slumped and she took her finger away from his mouth.

'Sometimes they double back, but it should be safe now.'

'How does she know that?' he thought.

She peered around the doorframe and down the street. Satisfied that the pulver had really gone, she turned back to him.

'Well, so it was boys you were arguing with; just lads in your street you were running away from was it?'

'Look, I have to get away. I can't get you into trouble as well, Alianna. Just let me go'

His voice had risen in panic. He was almost shouting. She slammed her hand over his mouth.

'Be quiet! We can't let them find you. You don't know what they're like.'

He shook his head free of her hand.

'What? And you do?'

'Darion,' she stared hard at him. 'Listen to me. You have got yourself mixed up in something that you are not ready for.'

'That's what Harrow told me.'

'And he's right,' she said. 'Now, stop loooking so grumpy. It's not your fault. It was all an accident, but now you *are* mixed up in it and...'

'Wait, wait. How do you know anything about...'

The question dried on his lips as Alianna stared at him.

'I know more about Harrow and Tur than you think.' She paused, still looking at him intently, as if wondering what to tell him next. At last she spoke again. 'The thing is Darion, it's no coincidence that we...'

Before she could say anything else, they heard more voices around the corner. Darion couldn't make out the words, but he definitely recognised one of the voices. His blood ran cold.

It was Jorian.

'Quick,' Alianna said. 'He must be helping those pulver search for you.' She looked around frantically. 'There. That way.' She pointed over his shoulder. 'That alley between the tall buildings. Move!'

She pulled at his arm and spun him around. He followed her at a run towards the alley.

Jorian and Alianna

He sped on through the alleyway. His head spun with questions. What had brought Alianna to that part of the city late at night? What had she meant about the thing he was mixed up in all being an accident? And what had she been about to say? It was no coincidence that... that? No coincidence that *what*? It was the second time that evening that someone had been prevented from telling him something.

'Wait here,' Alianna had stopped in the shadows. She peered around the corner, back the way they had come. 'I'll be back as soon as I can.'

She stepped back into the street again, leaving Darion alone.

'Hi there,' he heard her speak in a light, happy voice.

He heard Jorian answer her. 'Ali, what a surprise! What are you doing here?'

She mumbled her reply, Darion couldn't hear their conversation until Jorian raised his voice again to speak to the pulver.

'Carry on that way, if you see anything doubtful, use some excuse to arrest them. Tell them they've broken the curfew.'

'Right sir.'

'Straight away.'

Darion strained his ears and heard the pulver moving away. Alianna spoke again, but her voice was still too low for him to hear. What was she telling Jorian? He was desperate to find out. Jorian mumbled a quick reply then things went quiet.

Darion slowly leant forwards to peer around the doorway. He immediately wished he hadn't. What he saw felt like acid in his chest.

Jorian and Alianna stood just a couple of metres away. But there was no worry that Jorian might see him. His enemy was far too busy. Alianna's head was tilted back, her arms raised gently around Jorian's neck. His own arms gripped her tightly around the waist as she kissed him.

The sight was like a fist at his throat, but Darion couldn't tear his eyes away. How could he have been so stupid not to realise? He had been played like a fool. She wasn't his friend at all. She could never be his friend now, not if she was kissing Jorian. '*Why did it have to be him?*' he thought.

Then another thought struck him. She would tell Jorian he was there. He had to get away!

Darion looked back at the couple. He realised bitterly that they were still too busy to notice him. He slunk from his hiding place and started to walk swiftly away.

He broke into a run at the end of the alleyway. Tears were blinding him now as he sped out into the open street.

Bang.

Something hit the side of his head like a speeding carriage.

He dropped to the ground with a bolt of lightning shooting across his eyes.

'Got him.'

'Keep him down. Hold him.'

'Grab his legs.'

Darion tried to kick out against the hands that pinned him down. The movement shot another burst of pain pulsing through his head.

It was too late. They had him in a firm grip. He opened his eyes but just saw colours. It felt like three or four pairs of hands lifting him to his feet. Scratchy cords were being wrapped around his wrists. Tightly. He gasped, struggled, but more fingers held him securely. A hand grabbed his hair and pulled his neck back. The bright colours fireworked in front of him again.

'Led us a merry chase, didn't you? You Tenementerra rat.'

'Let's see how he likes a plunge in the sewer.'

''E's wet already, let's drown 'im properly this time.'

'No, leave him for Argolin and his boy.'

Darion felt his stomach heave with terror. He was going to throw up. They were taking him to Argolin...and Jorian.

The pulver began to drag him across the street. His head was hanging down. The colours started to merge into shapes in front of him. He saw cobbles dancing past his dragging feet, and polished boots marching along at either side of him. He felt vomit rise in his throat. It wouldn't be the first time that week he had thrown up on a pulver's boots.

Jorian. The thought of what his enemy might do to him plunged Darion into a despair worse than he had ever known. He sagged in defeat and allowed himself to be carried towards the tall buildings of the Variegatt.

Captured

But they didn't go to the Variegatt. Darion found himself half dragged, half carried through much more familiar streets. He was being taken close by the college buildings. Why would they bring him here? They had said they were going to Argolin, but surely he lived on the other side of the city?

Soon they reached the courtyard near to Harrow's classrooms. Darion tried to look up towards the windows, hoping that his teacher might be there, that he might be able to help. But he was forced away and through another set of doors on the opposite side of the building. Then, with a shudder, Darion finally realised where they were actually taking him.

They were going to Tur's chambers.

He started to scream.

'Quiet, or I'll shut your miserable mouth for you.'

He pulled back but the sets of arms holding him didn't even flinch. Darion's body sagged. He knew there was no use struggling. He let them drag him along, his feet tripping and stumbling as he went. In a few more minutes, they were outside Tur's door. Without even knocking he was taken inside.

They hurried through the room with the essence jars and the shelves of potions and mixtures. Right up to the door behind the tapestry at the far end of the room. This time, they did stop to knock.

After a moment the door creaked open. There stood Gretton Tur, with Argolin just behind him.

'At last,' said Argolin. 'Bring him in.'

Argolin moved to one side and Darion saw a metal table behind him. Ropes and chains hung down from brackets on the sides. He spun his head around to keep Tur in his line of sight. He wanted to be able to see what the old mage was doing, to see what he was *about* to do. Darion felt a cry of fear rising in his throat, ready to break out and show his terror.

Gretton Tur stood quite still by another, smaller table in the corner of the room. On top of it he had placed a number of syringes, needles, small knives and a bottle of yellow liquid.

'Sirs, I don't know what it is you think I've done, but I promise you I'm sorry.' His words burbled out of him in a rush, a senseless stream of sounds hoping for forgiveness, praying for mercy. 'It was all a silly mistake. I didn't mean to take the jar. It got mixed up with mine. I was just looking. Please, please, if I have done anything else to make you angry, I'm sorry. I'll do anything to make amends. Anyth –'

'Silence.' Argolin didn't move. His eyes bored straight into Darion as he spoke. 'Cover his face.'

'No sir, please! I wont tell them anything, honest. I didn't see anything anyway!'

'Do it now.'

He felt a movement behind him, heard a quiet rustling and then something rough and scratchy was thrown over his head. Everything went black.

Darion tried not to panic. He knew that it was no good struggling. The hands that held him down were too strong. Hard fingers bit deeply into his arms and legs. He felt himself being lifted roughly and dropped down onto a hard surface. He knew it must be the table that he had seen behind Argolin. He landed with such force that it winded him. His already bruised head knocked against the corner of the table.

His first fear was that he wouldn't be able to carry on breathing with the bag stifling him. Suffocating would be a horrible way to go. He clamped down on his panic again and forced himself to think.

The hands holding him twisted out his arms and legs until he felt the sharp corners of the table at his wrists and ankles. His heart quailed as he thought of the chains he had seen hanging down. Sure enough, a moment later he felt the cold metal of the cuffs against his skin. He heard a series of quick clicks as they locked into place on his limbs.

What could he tell them that would make them let him go? Already he knew that he was not brave enough to face torture. He would tell them *anything* to avoid being hurt. He did not feel like a coward; he did not hate himself for not being brave enough. He was scared for his life. This was something he simply could not change.

He heard a number of footsteps leading off in the direction of the door. They became more distant and then he heard the shush of the door closing and a small thump as it shut him in.

Everything had now gone silent in the room. He tried to slow his rapid breathing. This made him realise that he *could* still breathe. Even with the bag on his head. At least he wasn't going to suffocate. He managed to stop himself panicking. Instead he concentrated on listening to the room around him.

There was no sound for several seconds. He tested the strength of the chains holding him. It was futile. He knew that it would be. They had been tied too firmly. He could just about move his arms and legs a few centimetres, but that was all. He couldn't move his hand to the bag on his head to try to pull it off, or reach any of the fastenings to the cords and chains holding him down.

Anger started to take over now. He arched his back up and down on the table and pulled hard against his chains.

'You are advised to stop that.' The sudden voice made him jump. There *was* still someone in the room after all. They must have been watching him all this time.

'You will only hurt yourself unnecessarily,' the voice went on. 'That would be foolish. There will be enough pain for you soon. No need to add to it. Now hold still.'

The warning was sufficient to scare him into doing as he was told.

'Wiiy huff you mrort me hheurr?' he mumbled through the bag. 'Warra u wann frommee?'

'Hush, you will find out soon.'

The person didn't say any more. He thought it was Tur, but the bag muffled the sounds. It could have been Argolin. The room fell into a thick silence again.

Darion felt hot. He had heard about claustrophobia, and how some people couldn't stand being in a small space without it driving them into a paralysing fit of terror. He had never thought that he could be like that, but now he wasn't so sure. Another tingle of fear prickled his skin as if he had been plunged into cold water. The urge to fling himself about, to get free, was overwhelming.

Even so, he did as the voice told him. He forced himself to lie as still as he could. He felt another movement nearer to him this time. Darion jumped again. Something, no *someone*, touched his upper arm. He flinched back. Then he felt the skin of his shoulder being pinched by cruel fingers and a quick stab as something sharp was pushed into his shoulder. There was a buzz of pain that grew quickly outwards from his arm. The pain grew more intense and filled his whole body. His back spasmed and arched up off the table. Once. Then he drifted into unconsciousness.

*   *   *   *

Darion lay in the darkness. He was all alone. No one had come into the room to check on him for a long time. He didn't know exactly how long, but it felt like hours.

Every inch of him ached. His head pounded from dehydration – he daren't even think about the last time he had been given a drink of any kind.

He didn't want to be a hero any more. He didn't want to be brave like his father. He just wanted all of this to be over, and to be safe again.

He knew there was no shame in feeling this way. This was just the way he was. How he was made. '*Very few people are really brave,*' he thought.

He tried to swallow, but his mouth was too dry. Darion cleared his throat. It sounded strange, low and raspy. He wondered if he could still talk. He started to say, 'Is there anyone there?' but stopped straight away.

He couldn't speak the words.

It wasn't his voice.

It was a growl.

Before, he had been stretched out on his back, wrists and ankles tied at all four corners of the table. Now for some reason he had been rolled over onto his side. Both of his arms and legs were fastened together. He could feel thick straps across his chest and stomach. He tried to speak again, but something strange had definitely happened to his voice. It came out as a growl again. The knot of fear got tighter in his belly. What had they done to him? Had anything else about him changed?

Darion's thoughts whirled. If only he could get this hood off his head. It blocked out all of his vision. Well if he couldn't see anything, at least he could feel. He tried to move his fingers around. He couldn't do it. They seemed thicker and shorter somehow.

Darion remembered the stabbing feeling in his shoulder just before he had passed out. He knew that he had been injected with something. Was all of this just the after-effect of some drug that he had been given? He hoped so. He hoped that it wasn't anything worse.

He tried to move his fingers once more. His nails clacked against the table. This also felt wrong. He always bit his nails until they were ragged, chewed stumps. Now they felt even longer than the painted nails of the rich women he had seen in the Variegatt.

He shifted his position. The table felt more comfortable – softer somehow – as if someone had put a blanket under him to cushion him. Perhaps they had done it while he had been unconscious, when they moved him onto his side.

Darion moved again. He had the idea that it wasn't the table that was softer - it was him. He rolled his head inside the hood. Before he had been put to sleep the rough cloth had scratched his face, but now it felt protected by something smooth and comforting.

With a growing horror he realised what it was.

Fur.

His fur.

He cried out in shock. Instead of a scream, his voice came out in a terrified roar that echoed around the room.

He heard a door opening and rapid footsteps approached the table.

'He's woken up.'

'About time. He slept longer than any of the others.'

'The dose was heavier. It's no surprise.'

'He's squirming now, look at his head rocking.'

'Trying to escape.'

'He's panicking. Stop him. He'll injure himself.'

'Not important. Check the fastenings. Make sure he's secure.'

'Yes, he's safe.'

'Take the hood off.'

Darion felt hands and fingers around the cords at his throat.

A new voice stopped them.

'Wait! Leave the hood where it is.' The hands moved away. 'Let me speak to him first.'

Darion recognised this last voice at once...

It was Gretton Tur.

He tried to shout out an insult to the old mage. It came out as a snarl.

'Please stop that Darion,' Tur said. 'I want you to listen to me very carefully.'

The calm, soft way that Tur spoke only made Darion more furious. He roared and started thrashing against his bonds.

'Please do not do that. It is useless. You are quite secure. You will only succeed in hurting yourself further.' Tur's voice was louder now to make himself heard over Darion's snarls. 'And please stop that noise.'

He ignored him and carried on flexing his arms and legs – they felt much stronger than usual – trying to get free.

'If you don't stop that we will have to sedate you again,' Tur continued. 'The drugs we give you next time will be even more unpleasant. Believe me, you would not want that.'

Darion whimpered in fear.

'But if you lie still then this will all be over very soon. You have helped us in important work. I know that you will not trust what I say, but you must. Believe me Darion, we don't *want* to hurt you. Now. Darion. Are you ready for us to take off this hood?'

Darion attempted what he hoped was a nod of agreement.

'Good. Well done. Now lie still.'

He felt fingers at the cords around his throat again. His instinct was to snap out, to tear at something with his fangs, but he did as was told. He didn't struggle. He was panting; his chest rising and falling rapidly against the table.

The hood came off.

At first he just blinked in the sudden glare of the lights. It took several seconds for his eyes to adjust. Things gradually began to slide into focus.

As his vision cleared the first thing he saw was a long mirror on a wheeled frame. It had been placed near to the table and tilted towards him so that he could see himself. He stared at his reflection. He had already guessed, but here at last was the final, terrible proof of what had happened to him. What stared back at him out of the mirror was the red and grey striped face of a pedjiaar.

Escape

He didn't know how long his heartbroken roaring lasted. Tur and the others had left him alone again while he sobbed and wailed. He thought he might have slept again, but he couldn't be sure.

He lay on his side, looking at his reflection in the mirror. But no, it wasn't *his* reflection anymore. Where his dark hair should have flopped over his forehead, the flattened ears of a big cat flicked and twitched.

His hands were now broad paws. Long claws curved from the pads where his bitten fingernails should have been.

He moved his gaze from the mirror to look down at the rest of his body. He twitched and saw muscles ripple under the striped fur.

Darion took a deep breath and his great chest heaved. His life and heart broken, he wept until a nightmare-filled sleep took him once more.

*   *   *   *

His dreams seemed to last for days. He wasn't Darion any more. He was a pedjiaar, a big cat. How could he live life like that? He could never speak to anyone again. Never talk to friends, never grow up and live a normal life. Never sleep in a bed, or even live in a house anymore. He hoped they would kill him soon. Get it over with. He might as well be dead. Darion Melgardes was no more. His life, who he really was, didn't even exist now. Whatever he had hoped for, everything he had wondered about himself, what sort of life he would lead, what sort of person he was, or ever wanted to be; all that was over. The horror, the terror of what that meant had him screaming - roaring – again. He wanted to hurt everyone. Wanted to lash out, use those claws at the end of what had once been his hands to scratch, cut, wound, kill. He woke himself up with his roaring. He lay there for a moment as the full, waking horror hit him once more. It wasn't a dream. In sheer frustration he lashed out, expecting the chains and ropes to hold him.

But they didn't.

Nothing held him.

He could move.

Panting, feeling the hard edge of the table with his whiskers, he raised his head. There was the mirror, still in front of him, and now he saw the belts and shackles had all been unfastened. The chains hung loosely down the sides of the table. The ropes pooled in loops on the floor.

Someone had crept in while he slept and unfastened them all. Someone had come here to help him escape.

Who?

Harrow? Matthien? Alianna? Huh, no, surely not Alianna. She loved Jorian.

Why hadn't they woken him up? Was this another trap? Had they done this so he would try to escape? To give them an excuse to shoot him? He began to imagine that there were pulver waiting outside the room, weapons ready and aimed to shoot him down as soon as he stuck his striped head around the doorframe. Moments ago he had been wishing for death, just wanting everything to be over. But now his heart began racing again. No matter who he was, *what* he was, he wanted to live.

Carefully, Darion tried to get up. He had been lying still for a long time. His muscles tightened with stiffness as he moved. His huge front paws felt clumsy as he hauled his body up to a standing position on the table. He stretched out his long striped back and gave a long growling yawn.

His nose twitched as a stale, sickly smell stung at his nostrils. It stank like the chemicals that Cleve Harrow used in some of his classroom experiments. Darion couldn't help an angry growl escape as he realised that was what he was now, just an experiment. But Harrow could not have done this to him, could he? No. Harrow had helped him to escape. He wanted him to get clear of the city. His conversations with his teacher came back to him in bits and pieces as memories of the last couple of days swirled around.

Shaking his head to clear it from the last effects of the drugs they had given to him, Darion jumped down to the ground. He was amazed at how lightly he landed. He'd worried about making a noise, alerting a guard, but he hadn't made a sound.

His broad head swung slowly around the room. Flickering yellow, his bright eyes scanned up and down to get a full picture of his prison. There was the table and chains where he had been held captive. He saw a strange contraption made of metal, tubes and wires sitting next to it. One of the tubes led to a sharp needle and others held cruel looking pincers and clips.

No time now to wonder about the horrors those things had been used for. He padded swiftly to the door. It was made of heavy, solid oak, but to his relief he saw that it had been left slightly ajar. Darion nudged against the opening with his nose. The door creaked and shifted. Pushing again, he felt it swing further open. Now there was enough room for him to poke his head out into Tur's workshop. He glanced around at the familiar shelves of equipment. Then he noticed the door at the other end of the room was also slightly open. He could see into the corridor beyond.

Darion moved quickly past the shelves and worktables. Reaching the second door he pushed his head through it. His whiskers twitched as they touched the edge of the door frame. It was as if he could see how wide the door was through the end of his whiskers. He sniffed and a burst of smells and stenches exploded in his keen nostrils.

There was no one in the corridor, so Darion padded out. He turned in the direction he knew would lead him out to the courtyard.

It only took a few moments to reach the courtyard door. Again it was wide open. He stepped out into the night-time air. But which night? How long had he been lying in that room?

At least he was in a part of the city he knew like the back of his hand. '*Like the back of my paw,*' he thought grimly.

He couldn't be seen. He had to stick to the shadows. Otherwise he was just like another of those animals roaming around the city, hunted by the pulver.

He thought back to that first hunt that he had seen; the day he had first met Matthien, Alianna and the rest of the people from the Variegatt. Then, the awful truth hit him.

That hunt was not to chase off a rogue pedjiaar. It was not merely to scare away a big cat that had been rooting around the bins of the city. No, it was to catch and kill an experiment that had gone wrong.

A young boy or girl like him. An experiment like him.

He thought abut the missing children from the Tenementerra. He remembered how many more silkefoxes there had been in the city recently, and how they had become so eager to stay close to the houses. '*Because they had come home,*' he thought with a pang. '*They wanted to be near their families.*' He recalled what Fasker had told him about how determined the pulver had been to kill the creatures. '*Because they weren't really silkefoxes,*' he thought to himself. '*They were missing children. More experiments that Gretton Tur needed to keep secret.*'

The more Darion thought about it the more it all clicked into place in his head. Jorian had been helping his father to cover up the mistakes of Tur's shapeshifting experiments. Darion's thoughts reeled at the evil of it all, the dreadful cruelty. He tried to remember how many young people had gone missing recently. How many other children had they used like him? And who else was involved? Alianna? He remembered the way she had kissed Jorian. Even his pedjiaar heart broke a little further when he thought about how she had betrayed him. And what about Matthien? He had also been on the hunt with Jorian that day. Was Matthien's friendship just a lie too?

He knew that he had to find someone he could trust. Then he had to try to make them understand what was going on.

Another thought struck him. Someone already knew. A number of these children, turned into pedjiaar or silkefoxes, had been released. Someone had helped some of them escape, just as they had helped him. That meant that someone close to Tur must have known for a long time about his experiments. Who could it be? Harrow? Matthien? Fasker even? Had one of them sent an ament spy to release the children? Would they have access to Tur's rooms? He had to find that person.

But first he had to get further away from his enemies.

He stepped out into the street. If he turned left at the end he could be at Harrow's house in under five minutes. Harrow would know what to do.

Darion padded forwards. But just as he reached the end of the street his keen nose twitched. A musky smell of wet hair, hot breath and old leather. His ears flicked at a tiny sound. The rattle of a harness. Horses!

He looked down the street. Jorian's horse was circling nearby. Darion tried to calm his panting breath. He mustn't be heard.

But the horse's own senses were keen as well. Its nostrils flared as it smelled him. It gave a whinney of fear and clattered backwards on the cobbles. Jorian was instantly on the alert. His eyes shot up and down the street. They fell on Darion straight away.

'Steady there Haggard,' he said to his horse. 'Steady boy.'

Darion's yellow eyes fixed on Jorian's hated face. He could have him out of the saddle in a single leap, he thought. His tail swished gently from side to side. He dropped into a crouch, ready to pounce.

But then he saw Jorian's leering grin. Darion knew he had made a mistake. Behind him he heard the 'clop' of more hooves. They had him surrounded!

'Carefully, Dross,' said Jorian. 'Bargoth, move to his left. Quickly now.'

So, two of them behind him. One moving to his left to block his escape down the main street.

His tail flickered again. Jorian's hands were still on his reins. He had not drawn a weapon yet. There was not a moment to lose. Darion leapt forwards, up towards Jorian. Haggard, his skittish horse, whinnied again and reared up, punching the air with his front hooves. Jorian himself had flinched down, avoiding Darion's attack. An arrow shot past his ear.

'Careful you fools,' yelled Jorian. 'You'll shoot me instead of him!'

Then Darion was away down the street, limbs and whole body at full stretch, faster than he had ever moved before, towards the gates of the city and the plains and forests beyond.

Another Hunt

He stopped at last as the morning sun showed over the hills. Jorian and the rest had managed to follow him all night. He could still hear them not far off.

His striped fur kept him hidden in the slanting light that came through the branches. Silently he dropped down onto his haunches to give himself extra cover in the undergrowth. It was the instinctive move of a pedjiaar done without a thought. Now and again he caught a glimpse of Jorian's horse. It came close by his hiding place. He could see Jorian's sharp spurs dig into the horse's side, making its flanks shiver and twitch. Darion's nose filled with the strong scent of the creature. His yellow eyes were the only thing that moved. They watched every movement of his enemies.

'Jorian, can you see him?' It was Bargoth's voice.

'Quiet you fool.'

Another horse approached. He smelt the different creature, and the sweaty, unwashed clothes of the second man. '*Dross,*' he guessed. His black nose wrinkled up in distaste, showing his white fangs.

It might have been this flash of white teeth in the undergrowth, so different to the camouflage of his fur, that caught their attention. It might have been the horse whinnying and dancing away as it sensed him that gave the riders a warning. Whatever it was, Darion knew that they had seen him.

Through the leaves and grass he saw Jorian freeze in the saddle. He was looking straight at him. Darion stared back. He didn't move. Jorian's hand came up slowly. The index finger was raised, and he motioned Bargoth to ride to the left. Darion glanced around. He realised what Jorian was going to do. Oh, they had been clever, he thought. While they chased him they had manoeuvred him into a deep cleft of ground between the trees. Only a few metres away a high rock face curved around to his right, blocking his path. It looked steep and jagged. Too difficult to climb. Bargoth was already responding to his master's command. He had moved his horse to Darion's left. Now he was cutting off any escape route back down onto the trail. Darion was trapped. From the corner of his eye, he saw Bargoth reach for his bow. Frantically he looked back to see what Jorian was doing. His old enemy's horse was stepping closer. In one swift, smooth movement Jorian had notched an arrow to his own longbow. The arrow was aimed directly at Darion's chest.

'Look at you,' Jorian sneered at him. 'You're terrified aren't you?'

Darion snarled. If he had still been himself, he would just have curled up and given in. But the pedjiaar anger in him, fed by fear, suddenly made him brave. He flexed his front paws. He would not let himself be taken, or killed, without a fight. His rear haunches shifted, preparing to pounce. 'Bargoth will probably get me,' he thought to himself, 'but at least I'll take Jorian down first.' Violent thoughts of claws ripping at flesh flooded his mind for a moment. He snarled.

'Careful, kitty,' Jorian teased. His fingers were tight around his bowstring. 'Ready Bargoth?'

Darion had a sense of the other rider getting closer on his left.

'NOW!' Jorian let loose his arrow. At the same instant, with a mighty roar, Darion leapt at him. He felt a stinging cut slicing against his side as he flew through the air. He knew the arrow had hit him, but it hadn't stuck deep. He felt it clatter out of him against a tree as he struck the side of Jorian's horse. It gave a terrified whinny, rearing on its hind legs. Jorian was a skilled rider, but it took all his strength to stay in the saddle. Darion's teeth flashed close to his attacker's leg, the horse reared higher, pushing the rider completely off balance.

Pedjiaar, horse and rider tumbled in a heap on the forest floor. Darion felt a blood anger surge in him and he plunged his teeth towards Jorian once more. Maddened with fear, the horse kicked itself away from the melee and galloped off. Jorian was left on the ground. He screamed. Darion's teeth clashed close by his enemy's face. Jorian's arms were around the thick fur on his throat. With all his strength he held Darion back.

'Kill him! Kill him, Bargoth!'

Darion snarled again. He lunged forwards to bite once more. He was closer this time. Jorian was growing weaker.

But then, another arrow whizzed past Darion's side.

'Got you, Tenementerra filth!' Bargoth's voice.

Darion had no time for the killing blow to Jorian. But there was no need. As he looked down Darion saw that the last arrow, meant for him, had struck his enemy instead. It still twitched in Jorian's chest. One of the Variegatt lord's hands reached up to pluck it away, but his fingers couldn't grasp it. There was a surprised look on Jorian's face as the light died in his eyes.

'Jorian?' He heard Bargoth's voice behind him. Then there was a gasp of shock and anger. He turned to see Bargoth notching another arrow to his bow. Dross had ridden up as well, his mouth hanging open as he saw his master's body. He reached for his own arrows. This time Darion knew they would not miss.

His animal instinct to escape from mortal danger was even stronger than the blood-lust he felt. It pulled him away swiftly. He careered through the trees, before Bargoth or Dross could let their arrows fly.

Eyes wide, legs leaping at full stretch, Darion ran on in panic. He twisted one side to another, jinking his way through trees. He could still hear Bargoth's voice behind him.

'Murderer! We'll tell the whole city *you* killed him!'

'There'll be a hundred of us hunting you by nightfall,' Dross shouted.

A step later, he felt the ground give way under his paws. A loose layer of pebble and sand at the edge of a steep slope skittered away down the hill, taking him with it. He struggled to regain his balance, but tumbled tail over paw down the slope. Thankfully it was not too deep, but he still landed heavily on his right flank when he reached the bottom. He twisted up onto his four feet again and limped on, growling with anger at every step. The fall had taken him farther away from his pursuers. He could only just hear them now. They were high up above him; their voices growing ever fainter as they searched in the wrong direction.

Darion sniffed the air and spun away from them, plunging even further into the forest.

Point Blank

H is lungs heaved for breath as he struggled to the edge of the trees. The hunters' voices had completely faded behind him now. He had got away but it had taken the last of his strength. He swung his head around and began to lick at the wound on his flank. His pedjiaar sense told him it was important to clean the wound so that it did not become infected.

It was still bleeding. It stung as his rough tongue probed the flesh. A couple of gutflies started buzzing around the cut. He snapped at them with his jaws and swished his tail to hurry them away.

He felt exhausted. The chase had worn him down more than he had realised. The terror of being hunted, the effort of putting every ounce of energy into escaping death, then the thrill of attacking and the smell of blood had all left him shattered. And Jorian. Jorian was dead! He closed his eyes. His muscles began to relax. It felt wonderful to let himself begin to drowse. Just a few minutes of sleep and he would feel better. His chest heaved an enormous breath and his mind drifted further away.

Then his nose twitched. Instinct again. A new scent drifted towards him through the air. It smelled of honeysuckle with a hint of spice. He wracked his memory to think where he had smelt such an aroma before. A twig snapped in the undergrowth nearby. At once he turned and began to leap away into the cover of the thicker trees. He had been a fool to stop here. They were on to him.

'Darion, wait!'

The voice came from behind him. He recognised it straight away. That, and the use of his name, brought him up instantly. He stopped, poised on his haunches, ready to flee again if he needed to.

'Please Darion, don't run.'

Still panting heavily from the chase he turned his broad head around. As he did, he remembered where he had last smelt that scent of honeysuckle and spice. Standing just a few metres away, with her bow notched and aimed directly at him, was Alianna.

'Please don't run,' she repeated.

He bared his teeth at her in reply.

'You have to trust me,' she said.

He wanted to yell back at her, '*Then stop pointing an arrow at me!*' But he knew that anything he tried to say would just come out as a roar of fury. His hunting cat brain told him to attack. The pedjiaar essence flowing through him meant that a big part of him didn't even recognise her as Alianna. It only saw her as a threat...or prey.

He realised how hungry he was. His whiskers twitched.

Alianna must have recognised this sign and tightened the bowstring even further. The end of the arrow wobbled slightly. He saw that her hands were trembling. He knew that he was quick enough. He knew that she was not like Jorian, or Bargoth. She would hesitate. Scratched, bruised and wounded as he was, he knew he could probably still escape, or attack her before she had chance to release the shot. Should he pounce, or run into the trees?

His whiskers twitched again. He couldn't stop them. So many things were now happening as a pedjiaar, without his thought, without his intention.

But there was still a small part of *Darion Melgardes* left. A part of him that held him back. A part of him that realised Alianna knew who he was; recognised that small part of him that wasn't a pedjiaar. Would she shoot him? Could she? Even if she was working with Jorian and his father, could she bring herself to do it?

The two remained where they were, staring at each other.

'Please Darion, don't move,' she said. 'You have to trust me.' Alianna lowered the bow slightly. Her eyes were pleading with him. 'Trust me.'

He relaxed and his broad, striped shoulders slumped. He stood in front of her, his head hanging down panting heavily.

She could see that he wasn't going to attack.

She raised the bow again and fired.

Betrayed

His first waking thought was one of anger. He wanted to scratch, bite and kill. Alianna had betrayed him. She had made him think she was a friend, but she was as bad as the rest of them. She *was* them! There was *no one* he could trust. *No one* was as they seemed. Everyone lied and pretended. They changed who they were, wore masks, hid their real selves; they would do anything to get what they wanted.

Darion felt dizzy and sick. His cuts stung, and he felt a deep ache in his leg where he had landed at the bottom of the ravine. It made him grimace in agony but he tried to get to his feet. It was then that he felt something wrapped around him. A blanket had been thrown around his shoulders. He felt a sudden cold wind blowing through the trees. He gripped the blanket more tightly with his fingers.

His fingers.

Not claws.

Fingers.

Darion looked down. He brought one of his hands up and looked at it. A boy's hand, covered in skin, with long fingers and chewed nails. *His* hand.

Darion's mouth hung open in astonishment.

'How are you feeling?'

He jumped at the voice. Alianna was sitting a little way off in a clearing by the trees. She had made a campfire and was about to light it. On the ground next to her he saw two small creatures. They looked like rabbits. She had already skinned the first one and now started to skewer its body on a stick.

She looked at him with concern. 'Are you ok?' she asked again.

'I'd be a lot worse if I hadn't been shot full of antidote,' he said. 'It *was* an antidote you fired at me I suppose?'

She nodded. 'The end of the dart was soaked in it. I'm sorry. It was the only thing I could think of. It was the only way I could get you back.'

That was a huge thing to think about. She had wanted to get him back.

'Am I forgiven?' she asked.

The way her voice had cracked a bit when she asked the question; the way she had turned away from him, her hair covering her face, made him feel as if something was melting in his chest.

'Well?' she said again. 'Am I forgiven?' She smoothed her hair away from her face to look at him. He thought he saw something wet on her cheek.

He nodded. She gave a quick smile and turned back to preparing the rabbits. The first was now roasting over the fire and she had started to skin the second one with a small, thin knife.

'Hungry? This will take about half an hour.'

'Great,' he said. His throat hurt, and his voice still sounded strange. But at least it was *his* voice; not a pedjiaar's growl anymore.

For the first time he realised that he was naked under his blanket. He blushed when he realised that it must have been Alianna who had covered him up.

As if in answer to his embarrassment she stood up from the fire. She went over to her horse. He watched her unwrap something from the saddlebags.

'You'd better put these on.' Alianna walked back to him carrying a bundle of clothing in her arms. She handed them to him.

He looked down at the clothes. There was a sturdy pair of thick riding breeches, a fine shirt made of pale blue silk and a leather jerkin.

'There are some boots by the fire,' she said.

'How did you know to bring...' The question died in his throat. He had too many questions.

'I'll stand over there.'

She moved off behind the trees.

As quickly as he could he scrambled into the clothes. They felt soft and comfortable against his skin. He had never worn anything like this before. He knew that the fabrics must be of the best quality. As he moved to the fire to pick up the boots he called across to where Alianna stood between two rowan trees. She had her back towards him and was gazing out towards the mountains.

'How did you know to bring clothes for me?' he asked again. All sorts of suspicions were swimming around in his head. He didn't want to have to think about any of them, but he knew that he needed answers. He had been tricked, hunted, transformed, shot at and kept in the dark for too long. He just wanted to know the truth now. Whatever it was; whatever it meant.

She still hadn't answered.

'Come on, tell me,' he insisted. 'You knew all along what had happened to me didn't you? Otherwise you wouldn't have set off carrying those clothes.'

He stared at her. She still said nothing.

'All along. You knew all along.' He swallowed hard.

'Yes. And all along I meant to help you. And the fact that I *did* bring the clothes should tell you that.'

He thought about this for a moment. It made sense, sort of. He was still angry at her, but she *had* helped him.

179

Something else occurred to him.

'What was the drug, the antidote, on that dart you fired at me?'

'Your essence.'

'What?'

'It was your own essence, Darion.'

'Where did you...? How did you get it?'

'I collected it on the night of the ball. Remember when I pinned the brooch to your costume?'

The memory filled his head in a jolt. He felt the world tilt underneath him as he realised how clever she had been.

'You got it when you pricked me with the brooch.'

'Yes. I'm afraid that wasn't an accident after all.'

'Why? I mean, how did you know that you would need it?'

'We *didn't* know.'

'Then why...'

'We didn't know *then*. But our work means that we can't take anything for chance. We have to look at all the possibilities and be prepared. For everything that we can.'

'Wait a minute...who do you mean by *we*?'

She held up her hand to stop him. 'I'm coming to that. Matt and I had already talked about how you might be of use to us in the future. He wanted to tell you straight away about the work that we were doing, but it was Cleve Harrow who told him to wait.'

'Just a minute. Your work? What do mean by *your work*?'

Darion thought back to that evening with Harrow and Fasker. He thought about what Harrow had been about to tell him. 'Your father was an ament, Darion.' Harrow had said to him. 'Like your n...' but Harrow had not been able to finish; the pulver were already racing up the stairs. Darion had been forced to escape through the window before he could hear anything else.

'Like your n...'

Darion now realised what the Cleve had been about to say. Darion looked at Alianna and whispered: *'Like your new friend.'* He carried on staring into her face. 'Harrow was about to tell me. You are an ament aren't you?'

Alianna nodded.

'I am an ament, and a spy, Darion. I work for the Select families. The Select of Beltheron are the only group of people with enough influence to speak out against what Argolin and the Guild are trying to do. Matthien works with us as well. That is why we were keeping an eye on you. That's why he kept turning up in your classes after we had met you in the forest. He volunteered. We wanted to watch you, to see if you might want to follow in your father's footsteps and join us.'

'Join you? Like my father?'

'You do know that your father was an ament spy too, don't you?' she asked.

He nodded 'Harrow did manage to tell me that, just before I escaped over the rooftops.'

'Yes, I thought he would. We thought you would be ready to join us you see, but there was no time to...'

His head was reeling. This was too much to take in.

'Wait a second. You were watching me, studying me all that time?'

She nodded. 'Remember a few nights ago when you were running from the pulver? How do you think we just happened to bump into each other in that huge city with all those streets?'

He shook his head. 'I don't know. I hadn't thought about it. I kind of had other things on my mind that night.'

'I had been following you. Ever since we realised that Tur's men were looking for you.'

'You knew they were looking for me?'

181

'You can thank Jorian for that.'

'What? Jorian was helping you as well?'

She shook her head. 'Huh, like *that* was ever going to happen! No, Jorian is his father's son through and through. He always acted with complete loyalty to the Guild, and to his father's wishes.'

'So how come I have Jorian to thank for you finding me?'

'I have been spying on Jorian for months. Almost a year ago the Select had a meeting with Harrow and the ament spies. They wanted me to get close to Argolin's family if I could. They thought that Argolin was making some deal with the Maraglar city merchants, and that Tur was fashioning a breed of shape-shifters to help him take over Beltheron.'

'But Lord Argolin was already rich,' Darion said. 'He could have just about anything he wanted. He was already one of the most powerful men in the city. Why would he want to do this?'

'Huh! You think being rich and powerful makes someone like that contented? There are many people, even more powerful than Argolin, who only think of more and more power. People like him are never satisfied, Darion. It's like a sickness, it's all they think about. They'll do anything they can to make sure they keep their power and money, to make sure no one else can get close to them.'

Darion thought back to the night at the great banquet in the Variegatt. All that wealth, all that luxury, more than he could ever have imagined. He knew that if that were his, he would do anything not to lose it.

Alianna saw his expression change. 'You realise they'll do anything to stay in control don't you?' she said.

He nodded.

'And so,' she continued. 'You must realise how important it is that we fight them. To try to stop them from hurting more and more people.'

Alianna dropped her eyes. She gazed down at her hands, which had begun to twist at a loose thread of her belt.

'Your father put himself in terrible danger more often than anyone else. If it weren't for him, we wouldn't know nearly so much about Argolin's and Tur's plans,' she said. 'He found out that children, young people from the tenementerra were being taken from their houses.'

Darion nodded. 'Yes, I'd worked that bit out for myself.'

'You see, Tur discovered a way to use essences in a new way. He found a way to shape-shift a creature completely. That's what Argolin and Tur started to call it: shifting. They found they could shift - change - a person or an animal into something else entirely. They could change their very *essence*, Darion. '

He gave a short, bitter laugh. 'I'd worked that out as well. After what they did to me.'

She nodded again and took a deep breath. 'This is going to be difficult for you to hear Darion,' she said. 'But when your father did find out just what was going on, we think Argolin's men killed him.'

Darion had started to suspect this already. But hearing someone else say the actual words made it real, not just some idea in his head.

'So you were going to find the right moment to tell me all of this, thinking I would want to join you, to revenge my father?'

She nodded. Her head dropped away from him. She turned and gazed at the ripples in the bend of the river.

Darion's thoughts tilted backwards and forwards. Was *nothing* in the world what he thought it was?

But he had news for her too.

'Alianna. There's something you need to know.'

She looked back at him.

'It's about Jorian.'

'What about him?'

'He's, you see, Bargoth, he...'

'What, Darion? Tell me.'

He took a deep breath. 'They were hunting me, Ali. There was an accident. Bargoth shot him. Shot him instead of me. He's dead, Ali. Jorian's dead.'

She didn't say anything. She just nodded silently. Her arms folded against her chest. Darion saw her begin to nibble her lip.

'Ali, are you alright?'

She turned away from him and stared downriver again. When she finally spoke, her face was bitter.

'He had it coming.'

'I'm sorry Ali.'

'Why? You didn't do it. I don't think I'd blame you if you had. There's no need to be sorry anyway. Not for him.' She shivered. 'No need at all.'

There was a long silence between them.

'I'm really tired,' he said after a couple of minutes. He felt he had to say *something*.

Alianna was still staring ahead of her at the river. 'That's normal,' she said. 'After being shifted I mean. A pedjiaar has so much more natural energy than a person. You have used up so much of your own energy over the last couple of days. Now there is nothing left. You need to rest. Get as much sleep as you can.'

Even as she said this he felt an immense yawn growing in the back of his throat. His eyelids drooped and he felt the weariness in every muscle of his body.

'There's so much more I have to tell you. So much you still need to know. But I'll let you sleep now,' Alianna said. 'Later, when you're feeling better, we can...'

But he was already snoring.

Back

He woke up to find her standing over him. He must have slept for a couple of hours because the sun had moved around the sky. It was now hanging down low over the mountains. Long shadows from the trees fell across his body. He shivered.

'We'd better get ready,' she said.

He climbed to his feet. Before he could think, he had already started speaking.

'Did you ever really like Jorian?' He knew it was a stupid question straightaway. Something like that shouldn't matter at all with so much going on. But he still needed to know.

She laughed out loud. '*Like* him? Really Darion, you can be a bit dull sometimes. How could I have liked him? He was a mean, arrogant bully.'

Darion knew that he would never get a better chance to own up to what he had seen in the street that night. If he didn't say something now, then the chance would never come again. '*What does it matter now anyway,*' he thought to himself. '*After everything else, this should be easy.*'

He took a deep breath. 'Alianna?'

'Yes, what?'

'Do you remember when...' He struggled to continue.

'Yes? Go on.'

'I saw him. With you. A few nights ago in the street. I was looking when... when...I saw you kiss him.'

Her smile faded. 'Oh Darion, I wanted him to trust me. He and his father both thought that a *marriage-match* as they called it would be good for their family,' she paused and shuddered at the idea. 'And it was my duty to keep in his confidence. I *hated* doing it.' She stared hard at him. All signs of smiling or laughter had gone. Now her lips were pressed tightly together, as if she was still fighting against the memory of that kiss.

Darion couldn't meet her stare. 'I'm sorry, I'm stupid. I shouldn't have said it.'

'I had to forget who I was,' she went on. 'Pretend that it was someone else, not me at all. It was horrible.'

There was silence all around them. It was so thick that Darion felt he couldn't move.

Then Alianna spoke again. The corner of her mouth twitched in the beginning of a smile.

'Were you jealous?'

He didn't say anything. He didn't even move.

'Oh Darion, you *were* weren't you? Honestly. Boys *never* understand.'

She moved closer to him. Darion felt his stomach flip over.

Her hand started to move gently up to his face.

'Darion, I don't want you to ever feel that I...'

Her eyes moved away from his and she glanced behind him, over his shoulder. She grinned.

'Come on,' she said. 'I'll tell you the rest when we get back.' She dropped her hand and turned away. She started gathering her things together.

'Back?'

'To the city of course, back to Beltheron.'

'But how?' he asked. 'It's miles and miles from here.'

She smiled at him and pointed into the sky behind him. Then he heard a steady beating high in the air. He turned and looked up.

Swooping down from the mountainside came a huge draccen. It curved in the air and dropped towards them. Darion could see the figure of a man riding on the shoulders of the winged beast. The man held on tightly with one hand and waved down at them delightedly with the other. Darion squinted into the low evening sunlight as the draccen flew closer. Then his mouth dropped open in astonishment as he recognised who was riding it. It was his teacher, Cleve Harrow.

Carccen Firetongue

The draccen landed in the clearing next to them and Darion had to step backwards quickly. The wings beat close to his head. He could feel the hot air from its mouth swirl around his ears.

Cleve Harrow swung his leg across the neck of his steed and jumped to the ground. The draccen made a snickering, whickering sound in its throat. Steam vented from the narrow flaps along its neck.

'It's alright,' Cleve Harrow said. 'She is quite safe.'

Darion stepped forwards. The draccen unfurled its long neck and the head swung down towards him. He reached out his hand and tentatively stroked the creature's flank.

The draccen's skin was cold and leathery. His fingers flinched back in surprise. He had expected it to feel hard, or slimy, but the skin was more like a smooth fabric under his touch.

The draccen's lidless eyes looked into his own. He saw a tiny spark deep in the centre of the iris. It grew larger as if in recognition, or friendship, as their glances met. As he watched the flicker of flame there, it looked as though there were fires burning deep inside the draccen's body.

This light made him want to carry on staring into the creature's eyes. It seemed to draw him in. Like the welcoming fire in the hearth at home on a winter's night, it offered him peace and comfort. He surrendered to the feeling and in a moment the only thing he could see were the beast's ancient eyes. Darion shook his head, trying to clear the hypnotic effect. He felt himself stagger and realised he had been about to fall over. Had the draccen begun to put him into a trance he wondered? It was strange how he had always imagined the draccen to be fearful, dangerous beasts. But standing next to this one he had never felt so safe, so protected.

He realised that it hadn't just been looking into his eyes, returning his own gaze. It had been looking deep inside his heart, searching out the truth of his feelings, understanding him and who he really, *really* was. In those few moments it had seen all of his hopes and fears, his cowardice and failures. The thought made a shudder run through him.

The draccen turned away and began addressing Cleve Harrow in a series of low, sibilant hisses and scratchy sounds. The Cleve replied with his own guttural rasps and whispers.

'He can speak to it!' Darion murmured under his breath. He turned to Alianna. 'He knows how to speak draccen.'

'Of course,' Alianna smiled. 'They understand each other perfectly.'

It seemed that this was true. Harrow stopped speaking and the draccen lifted its head and shook it in a long, slow, serious nod of agreement.

Darion's head swam with disbelief. He had never even imagined that these creatures could communicate. He thought that they were just wild beasts acting on instinct. He assumed they were without reasoning, that they couldn't understand any kind of human thought process. But then he remembered the strange mixture of thoughts and emotions that he had experienced when he had been changed into the pedjiaar; that swirl of feelings had been totally different to what he was used to, but they were still feelings. Human feelings like fear, anger and a need for revenge. His pedjiaar feelings had been more intense though. As strong as the sour taste of lemons in your mouth, or a punch in your stomach.

Not just feelings either, he realised. He remembered how his pedjiaar self had made rational decisions about how to escape. It had done it much more easily than Darion – as himself - could ever have done. Perhaps it wasn't so unusual for the draccen to be able to think and converse with Harrow.

Cleve Harrow stepped away from the draccen. He turned and began walking towards Darion and Alianna.

'Is there any of that meat left? It smells too good to waste.'

The cooking fire had just about burnt out. A few wisps of smoke still hazed up into the sky that was now turning pink behind the mountains.

Alianna managed to scrape a few scraps of cold meat from the carcass of the second rabbit they had been eating earlier. She wrapped them in a cloth and handed them to the Cleve. He wolfed them down hungrily.

'That's good,' he mumbled through the mouthfuls. He started to lick his fingers and wipe them on the cloth.

'We will have to go soon,' he said. 'Darion, kick over the last of those embers there. Make sure the fire is out properly.'

Darion started to kick earth over the smoking pile of blackened wood. 'Cleve,' he said. 'Alianna told me that you wouldn't have known nearly so much about Argolin's treachery if it wasn't for my father.'

'That's true, Darion, he was a great help to us.'

'But Argolin and Tur just carried on with their experiments anyway,' Darion interrupted. 'So what good did any of this do?'

'Argolin would not have stopped no matter what,' Harrow continued. 'And Gretton Tur was bent upon serving him. He was compelled to carry on with his experiments.

It was a matter of pressing urgency to him. Together the two of them had become so powerful, they held such a sway over the councils that Argolin would have been able to turn aside any of our attempts to stop him.'

'Exactly! That's just what I mean. So what was the point of it all? If what my father found out wasn't going to stop Argolin's plans; if Tur was just going to carry on with his experiments and keep on taking children and, and...' Darion fell silent again as he thought about what Tur had done to him. His eyes stung at the memory of looking into the mirror and seeing his body shifted into the shape of the pedjiaar.

Harrow nodded slowly. 'It *is* hard to understand,' he said. 'Sometimes it can all seem pointless. But your father's discoveries allowed us to prepare ourselves. We knew we couldn't stop their monstrous actions, but we could turn our attentions to the best ways of preventing much of the damage they were causing. We could stop *some* of the pain.'

'It still doesn't seem like much,' Darion grumbled. 'Not enough for my father to give his life for. Just for things like...'

'For things like the antidote Alianna shot you with,' the Cleve interrupted.

Darion's hand moved to his side and he flinched with the memory of the dart going in.

'Who do you think mixed that for her?' Harrow asked.

'I suppose you did?'

'That's right. The antidote that saved you was brewed from your blood in our very own classroom. But we would not have known how to create that without the information about Tur's experiments which was gathered by your father. So don't be too quick to say that your father's life was wasted. His discoveries saved you Darion. And they will continue to save many more. Think of that.'

Harrow began to move back towards the draccen. She had settled down on her haunches now, waiting patiently, her wings curled around her long back.

'You see boy,' said Harrow. 'We are not teaching essence students so that they can serve and work for the Variegatt lords; we are doing it so that we have a way to *fight* them.

'Now, with that in mind, we mustn't lose any more time. We are already deep in shadows and the sun won't last much longer. Carccen Firetongue will take both of you directly to the Variegatt. She flies swiftly and she will see you safely home.'

Darion gestured towards the draccen. 'Is that its name? Carccen Firetongue?'

'It is, and she comes from an old and honourable family of draccen. We are honoured to have her help.'

Carccen's eyes narrowed into thin, bright gold slits as if she were smiling.

'Alianna, you mustn't speak to anyone on your return,' Harrow continued. 'Take the boy back to your home, and hide him somewhere in your rooms. Wait for my instructions. I still have work to do, another journey to make before I can come back to the city. I have…' he paused, his eyes flickering around. 'I have suspicions which I need to confirm. So, until I return, avoid everyone. Even your family, if you can.'

He looked at them both, then repeated his warning. 'Remember, speak to *no one*.'

Alianna nodded. She turned towards Darion and smiled encouragement. 'Come on, I've always wanted to ride a draccen.'

She hurried towards Carccen Firetongue and spoke to her.

'With your permission, my noble friend.'

Alianna bowed down low. Straight away, the draccen dropped her own head, opening her wings slightly. 'It's, I mean, *she's* curtseying,' Darion realised. His jaw dropped.

Just how many more surprises and secrets were going to be revealed to him today?

Carccen Firetongue made a rasping sound as he stepped closer. Her mouth grew wide, grinning at him, like a long lost friend saying hello.

Harrow glanced towards the lowering sun on the red-tinged mountaintops.

'It will be late by the time you arrive in Beltheron,' he said. 'Carccen can fly you high over the walls to escape the curfew. I'm hoping you can hide in the darkness, and there will be fewer people around to question you.'

These words made Darion even more nervous. It seemed his adventures were far from over.

'Come, we mustn't wait another moment.' The Cleve hurried them towards Carccen Firetongue. She obligingly dropped one of her shoulders to allow them to climb up onto her back.

'Are you not coming with us, Cleve?' Darion asked.

'Not now. As I have told you I have another journey to make first.'

'But how will...'

'Enough questions.' Harrow smiled at him. 'If you had been so full of curiosity in your classes my boy, you might have understood a little more about what is now happening around you.'

Darion blushed.

'Don't worry about me,' Harrow continued. 'If all goes well I will see you soon.'

Alianna was already astride the draccen's shoulders. She reached down towards Darion to help him up. In a flash he remembered the first time they had met and how she had helped him up onto her horse to join in the pedjiaar hunt. How he wished he were back there now, that he had never got himself mixed up in all this madness.

Too late for wishing now though. He was already sitting astride the wide back of Carccen Firetongue. She spread her leathery wings and leapt up into the scarlet sunset.

The City Attacked

Carccen carried them smoothly through the clouds. After what seemed like just a few minutes, her left wing dipped and she started to drop out of the darkening sky. Through the gathering shadows Darion saw the evening lights studded on the rounded walls of the Cittegare below them. The last wisps of thinner cloud disappeared as they dropped lower and he could make out the shape of streets as more and more lanterns were lit. It was like looking down onto a huge, living map of the city. He noticed the ragged tangle of streets that made up the Tenementerra. As they dropped closer, he tried to work out which was his street. It was strange, seeing his home from up here. It didn't look real, more like a coloured diagram from one of Harrow's text books.

Then something else caught his attention. Ragged lines of smoke rose up from the city walls to the north of the Tenementerra, out beyond the markets where they spread out into the narrow, crowded streets.

It wasn't just smoke. Darion's heart leapt as he realised. Even further away, towards the Variegatt, he could see flames starting to flicker from high windows in the turrets and towers of the great hall. The building was on fire!

He moved his hand and grabbed Alianna's shoulder.

'Look, down there.'

She followed his gaze. Both of them leant out over the draccen's beating wings to try to catch a glimpse of what might have happened.

As they flew closer to the great hall, they noticed that a large section of the city's outer wall had been destroyed. Stones and crumbled rock had fallen in a wide area around the gates to the Variegatt. Black smoke, the thickest Darion had ever seen, bloomed into the air around it.

'Carccen, can you take us closer?' Alianna shouted into the draccen's ear. Carccen rasped a reply. She made a sudden turn to fly them over the ruined walls. The black smoke choked them and stung their eyes as they strained to look. The wind whistled in their ears, whipping their hair into their faces.

'It's been blown up,' Darion said.

'Looks as if it was a powerful bomb,' Alianna replied.

'Who would want to attack the city?'

Alianna shook her head. 'That explosion came from *inside* the city,' she said. 'look at the way the stones are spread out onto the plain.'

He looked. Beyond the Variegatt walls was a wide stretch of sand leading to the first trees on the edge of the forest half a kilometre away. Through the smoke he saw the shattered stone fanning out over the sandy earth in front of the walls. Alianna was right. The explosion had come from inside the Variegatt.

'We're too late,' he whispered. 'Someone has betrayed our city.'

She shook her head. 'Maybe not. Some of our ament spies have been urging us to make a strike against Argolin for several days. This could be their work. The fight back against the Guild might have begun! Come on, Carccen, take us down. Let's find out who's...'

The rest of her words were stolen by the wind as Carccen Firetongue turned in the air and began a fast dive through the smoke and gathering darkness. Down they flew towards the smoking remains of the city.

They swooped lower and lower. Darion saw roofs and chimney stacks rushing by just below them. They whizzed past dizzyingly fast. Carccen levelled out a couple of metres above the smoky rooftops. Alianna turned her head towards him.

'We'll make straight for the Variegatt,' she said. She leant forwards and spoke directly into the draccen's ear. 'Carccen,' she said. 'Can you take us to that house over there? The one with the large courtyard?' She pointed to an elegant looking building a couple of hundred metres away. It stood next to the building of the great hall itself. The house had dozens of windows and a luxurious garden surrounded by a high wall. Darion recognised it from the evening of the banquet.

'That's Matt's house,' he said.

She nodded.

'Can we get in without anyone seeing us though?' asked Darion.

'We may not have a choice. Things have already got out of hand,' she replied. 'We might find ourselves in the thick of things before Harrow gets back.'

As they approached Matthien's house, they heard two shots ring out below them. Darion felt a fireball whip past his head. He clutched at Carccen's neck.

'They're firing at us,' he yelled.

'No, really?' came Alianna's sarcastic reply. She was already scanning the streets below to see where the shots had come from.

Another burst of light erupted to their left. Carccen Firetongue shrieked in alarm and spiralled in the opposite direction. Then she dipped suddenly to the left, dropping her wings under her belly. They began to plummet to the ground. For a moment Darion thought that she had been hit by one of the fireballs. The rooftops streamed past and the ground loomed closer. He closed his eyes and waited for the impact. He knew that in a moment they must either hit the earth or crash into one of the buildings. He breathed a sigh of relief as Carccen's wings opened wide again. She gave an excited cry and straightened her flight. They were safer now, she had flown them below the line of fire.

'The shots are coming from the great hall,' said Alianna. 'They got there before us.'

'Who?' he asked

'I just saw some blue cloaks: they're pulver guards,' she said. 'Many of them are loyal to the ament. They work with us against Argolin. I bet they are the ones who blew up the city wall too.'

'Then why are they firing at us?'

'They're firing at Carccen, not us. Remember the night of the party? Who arrived riding on draccen?'

Her meaning hit him straight away. 'Of course, they see a draccen flying overhead and they think we're from Maraglar. They think we've come to help Argolin.'

'That's right, and as the fighting's still going on, we'll be just as dead if we're shot by an ament's arrow or blown up by a pulver firebomb as we would by any other.'

'We should still try to find Matt,' Darion said. 'He might need our help too.'

She nodded. 'I want to talk to Matthien anyway. I need to tell him about everything that's been happening to you.'

'But the Cleve told us not to speak to anyone.'

She nodded. 'I know. But it's not just anyone, Darry. It's Matthien we're talking about. And this is desperate. Harrow didn't know we would find the city already under attack. Whatever he wants to keep quiet about, its too late. We can't wait for him; we need help *now*.'

*   *   *   *

It began to rain heavily as Carccen flew down into the courtyard of Matthien's father's estate. Her flight was guided by the flickering torches placed around the stone walls. The rain thickened as they descended. Carccen splashed down, shattering the reflected torchlight in the muddy puddles. Darion and Alianna slid off her back. Alianna bowed down to the draccen, 'Thank you Carccen Firetongue,' she said. 'We are in your debt. Your family is our family.'

The draccen tilted her head and gave a high whinnying sound in reply. Darion copied his friend's bow then turned to follow her as Alianna raced towards the doors.

'I don't think we were seen,' she said. 'Harrow was right, late evening was the best time to arrive. Now we just have to...'

Alianna stopped abruptly. She gave a short, gulping gasp and dropped to the ground. Darion thought she must have slipped on the wet cobbles of the courtyard. He moved forwards to help her up.

'Steady Ali. Here, let me help y...'

There was a pool of blood spreading out by her head. 'Alianna?' He heard the wet slap of an arrow hitting him a second before he felt the stabbing jolt in his side. The force of the blow spun him around. The arrow had struck him just below his ribs, but the pain seemed to shoot up his back and down behind his knees in the same instant. He crumpled to the floor and his head struck the cobbles. The last thing he saw as his vision faded was Alianna's face as she lay on the ground next to him. Her eyes were wide open and unmoving in the rain.

*   *   *   *

He must have been unconscious for just a few moments. An angry screech from Carccen Firetongue woke him. The tearing pain took his breath away. People began shouting nearby.

'Get that draccen! Shoot it!'

'Kill the monster!'

He could feel the pulse of Carccen's huge wings in the air as she circled just metres above his head. She cried again in fury and he opened his eyes in time to see her lunge down towards two bowmen. They were standing on the steps of Matthien's house. As Carccen flew closer to the bowmen Darion heard the voice crying out the order once more: 'The ament are both down, now kill their beast!'

They both struggled to get new arrows notched to their bows. Too late. Carccen's breath engulfed them. The air around the bowmen distorted in heat haze and a second later, flames burst from their clothing. Their screams were terrible. Darion saw a third figure standing further up the steps. Not quite a full grown adult, but a young man of maybe fourteen or so. As the other two men crumpled in shrieking flames their younger companion turned away. He jumped up the final stairs and disappeared back into the house. The large oak door slammed closed behind him. Darion couldn't see who it was through the heat haze, but he had recognised the voice giving the orders to shoot at Carccen.

It was Matthien's voice.

His head swam. He struggled to make sense of everything that had just happened. *Matthien?*

Carccen Firetongue landed next to him. She gave a concerned warbling rasp in her throat and nudged at Alianna with her snout. Darion turned his attention back to her.

'Alianna? Alianna, can you get up?'

There was no reply. She lay motionless on the wet stones. Carccen began to wail. She threw back her head and howled.

Fire lashed from her throat as the great draccen screamed into the night sky.

A rage unlike anything Darion had ever known swept through him.

He felt down at his side. The arrow had gone through his tunic and pierced his body. He winced again but carried on carefully moving his fingers around the wound towards his back. He could just feel the tip of the arrow poking out under his skin. As he touched it he felt another stab of agony. This time the pain pulsed up his back. It was so strong and sudden that he felt it would push his eyeballs out of their sockets. He shook his head with determination and carried on. As he moved his fingers he could tell that the arrow had almost missed him and punched through just a few centimetres of flesh. He realised that the wound felt much worse than it actually was. If he could pull the arrow out it would hurt like hell itself - he quailed at the thought of how much - but he was confident it wouldn't kill him.

He moved his hand back to where the arrow had entered his side. Taking a deep sobbing breath, he pulled. A burst of screaming pain like hot needles almost made him pass out again, but the arrow was free. He felt a fresh surge of hot blood seep through his tunic, but he ignored it.

Carccen Firetongue was still at his side. Her hot breath warmed him in the rain that drenched them both.

'Carccen,' he gasped. 'We can't stay here. Can you lift me? Can you get me out?'

She gave a grunt. Her snout pushed under his shoulders. With her broad head against his back she managed to lift him into a sitting position. At last he managed to grab hold of her neck and stand up. All the time she nudged and nuzzled with her head to help him. In another few moments he had scrambled onto her back. He held on tight. The draccen gave a cry of triumph and wheeled up into the sky with a single flap of her wings.

As they began to rise out of the courtyard he took one last look down towards Alianna.

It was hard to tell through the swirl of smoke, but for a moment he thought he saw her move. He blinked, tears as well as the smoke now blurring his vision. Had he been mistaken? They were getting further and further away. The wind gusted, taking away the smoke, and for just a moment he could see clearly. He was right! Alianna *was* moving! He watched her struggling to her feet.

'Carccen, we have to go back.'

The draccen shook her huge head. The action almost tipped him from her back. She screeched and carried on flying upwards, away from the flames.

'Carccen please! Alianna is alive. We can't leave her.' Tears stung his eyes. He pounded with his fist on Carccen's shoulder. 'Take me back down. She's your friend too, Carccen. Please, I'm begging you.' Carccen was moving upwards so swiftly that they had already left the highest turrets of Matthien's home far below. At Darion's order she folded one wing, wheeled around and swooped back down towards Beltheron City.

But before they had reached the top of the mansion's courtyard walls, the shots began again. Carccen dipped suddenly to one side, one wing tucked under her belly, the other flapping wildly, and Darion felt a fireball whizz past his neck. He clutched even more tightly at Carccen's side.

'They're firing at us, again!' he yelled.

Carccen gave a sarcastic screech as if to say; 'Yes, so you keep saying!'

Both were gazing down, searching the mansion buildings to see where the shot had come from. Darion couldn't see anyone. Not even Alianna. She had gone.

Another burst of light erupted to their left. It sent a gust of hot air that blew Carccen Firetongue off her course. She spiralled away from the threat of more explosions, looping upwards back into the sky. Then another arrow sped past the scales of her ear. With a twist that threatened to throw Darion off her back, the draccen lunged down again. Trying to get out of range of the fireballs, she dropped rapidly on the other side of the walls of Matthien's house, safe from whoever was shooting at them.

They found themselves dropping into a side-street. Here, the buildings on either side were crowded closely together. Carccen didn't have space to spread her wings. She couldn't control her descent. They landed heavily on the cobbles. They were now slippery with the rain. Her clawed feet skittered and slid underneath her. One of her shoulders struck hard against a stone wall.

Darion felt the breath knocked from his lungs. Carccen looked around her frantically. In these narrower streets it was impossible for her to turn around comfortably. She hissed nervously and dropped her shoulder. Darion guessed that she meant him to get down. He slid his leg over her flank and tumbled clumsily to the ground. He jumped up and looked around for a way to escape. He knew that they might only have a matter of moments before their attackers found them.

There was a gateway at one end of the street. Carccen nudged him towards it with her snout. She hissed and pushed harder. She was telling him to run that way. 'She must know it's the way out,' he thought. He didn't have time or energy to argue. The draccen had proved herself many times over. She was the only thing left that he could trust.

She gave him one final, encouraging push and flapped her wings. Leaping up on her back legs until she was standing almost vertically, Carccen launched herself into the sky. She gave a loud screech as she showed herself above the rooftops again. 'She's drawing attention away from me,' he thought. 'Bless her. She's going to draw their fire. She's giving me a chance!'

Sure enough a series of arrows whistled towards Carccen from behind the houses on the other side of the street. A sudden, fiery breath from Carccen and the arrows burst into flame, before curling away diagonally into the air like smoke escaping from a chimney in the wind.

'Go on,' he whispered under his breath. 'Go on, Carccen. Get away from them!'

Darion watched for a few seconds more, until she had flown further off and he was satisfied she was now out of range.

He heard shouts around the corner behind him. No time to lose. Darion turned and ran towards the gateway that Carccen had shown him.

As he reached the gateway Darion saw that one of the explosions must have set fire to the house near the end of the street. Windows exploded outwards into the street in front of him. The glass from one of them shattered just paces from where he stood. A gout of flame punched into the air from the gap in the building. It was followed by a shroud of thick smoke that engulfed him. he choked and stumbled his way forwards. He had to get to the gate.

Smoke and shadows swirled around him.. They confused the shapes and distances between objects. Darion felt he was struggling through a continually moving maze.

At last he reached the gateway. It was huge and made of a solid blackened metal. He would have had no way of opening it on his own, but he saw it must have already been hit by one of the explosions. It was hanging at an angle, one set of heavy bolts twisted out from the stone wall above his head. There was just enough space for him to crawl through the gap.

As soon as he squeezed through and looked around him, he recognised his surroundings once more. He was standing before the great hall of the Variegatt. There was the staircase leading to the huge doors he had walked through to the party. That seemed like a lifetime ago now. He made out the shape of someone moving down the stairs towards him. He held a flaming arrow notched to his hunting bow.

Darion squinted through the smoke. He tried to make out the figure, but the jagged light of the fires distorted the face. They threw deep shadows across the forehead and turned the eyes into caverns of darkness.

Then another sky-wide crack of lightning killed all the shadows for a split second. The place was filled with light. In that moment, Darion saw who stood in front of him. He knew now who had shot Alianna, and he also knew who had betrayed them all to Argolin and Gretton Tur.

It was Matthien. And the flaming arrow notched to his bow was aimed directly at Darion's heart.

They stood facing each other while all around them the Variegatt crumbled.

Another Betrayal

M atthien didn't fire at first. He held the bow steadily, still aiming at Darion's chest. He motioned with the burning tip of the arrow to a doorway on Darion's left.

'Move!'

Darion stayed where he was. His eyes were locked onto Matthien's face. It was difficult to read the emotion there, it was so heavily disguised by dirt, smoke and flame.

'I said move, you shred!'

The arrow tip moved sideways again, more violently this time.

Darion looked to where Matthien was pointing. He could see an open doorway in the outside wall. He guessed it must lead back into the part of the Variegatt where Matthien lived. Back into the heart of his enemy's home.

'Argolin will want to see you.'

'It's not the first time I've been threatened with an arrow this week,' Darion said.

'Do as I say or it will definitely be the last,' Matthien replied.

'Really Matthien? Huh, you sound like you've been taking threatening lessons from that ridiculous Jorian.'

Darion was amazed to hear these words and realise that it was he who had said them. He felt braver than he ever had before. For a brief moment he wondered why. Probably because he had nothing else to lose, he thought. Yes, that was probably it. Now he could say anything and it wouldn't make any difference at all. He knew he would be killed anyway. He might as well tell Matthien what he thought of him before he died.

'I won't tell you again.' The arrow gestured to the doorway a second time. 'Move, NOW!'

Darion did move. But not towards the doorway. Instead, Darion rushed straight towards Matthien, his new courage growing inside him with every step.

'I am warning you,' Matthien said. 'Do as I say now, or...'

'Or what?' Darion shouted as he moved. 'You'll shoot me down in my tracks?' He advanced so suddenly, his outburst was so unexpected, it was enough to make Matthien hesitate. The arrow tip wavered. Darion's voice grew louder. 'What? You'll kill me like a pedjiaar? Like Bargoth did to the one you were hunting that day you first met me? Hey?' He moved another step closer. 'Hey?' Another step. His arms came up, his hands in fists. 'HEY?'

Matthien was caught completely off balance. It had only taken Darion a few seconds to close the gap between them.

'Alianna told me that you volunteered with the ament to come to the classes to look after me,' Darion went on. 'But you were really keeping an eye on me for Argolin weren't you?'

Matthien stared at him. 'Very clever. Worked it all out have you?'

'I think so,' said Darion. 'As soon as I thought about it properly I knew it must have been you who told Argolin that I had been in Tur's rooms. You saw that new jar and knew immediately that it wasn't mine. Did you go straight to Tur's rooms yourself after you left the class? Hey? Did you search his shelves and find my broken jar?'

His voice became a snarl. 'And did you tell them that I would probably have told Vershan all about it? Was it you who ordered them to kill him too? Was it? Hey? HEY?'

Now he was within arm's reach of the arrow tip. It still flickered with fire.

'Yes,' said Matthien. 'It was me. But there's something you haven't worked out yet. Didn't you wonder who it was that untied you from Tur's table and helped you to get out of his rooms?'

Darion hesitated.

'That was me too. In fact, it was my idea to release all of the children after we'd shifted them into pedjiaar or silkefoxes. Those who survived the shift anyway. We didn't need them, you see. They were just the early stages of Tur's experiments. Oh we could have just killed them. But having rogue animals wandering the streets of Beltheron was useful to us. We could blame them for the missing children. And of course it gave Argolin another excuse to increase the power of his Guild guards. The city needed protecting.' Matthien sneered, his fingers pinching tighter on the bowstring. 'When Alianna decided she wanted to come with us, to help us scare them off, it was awkward of course. We had to make sure she didn't see the actual kill. But how much fun it was to hunt them!' He laughed into Darion's face. 'She didn't understood what was really going on.'

'I understand you perfectly now,' said Darion. 'I understand the very *essence* of you Matthien. I know you right down to your bones.' He gave a short, bitter laugh. 'Huh. Maybe I'm a better hunter than you after all.'

Matthien's fingers moved again on the bow. But it was too late.

Darion swiped his arm sideways. It made contact with the burning arrowhead just as Matthien released the bowstring.

With a terrible hissing, Darion felt the heat of the arrow singe its way along his arm. But it was only for a moment. The arrow flew off, wide of its mark. Darion brought up his other arm. The hand clenched into a fist and struck at Matthien's chin. Matthien was already ducking away. He cursed himself for his mistake as he swung the bow around. It struck Darion painfully behind the ear.

The force of the blow dropped Darion onto one knee, but his fist had already made contact with Matthien's face and the older boy also staggered back, off balance.

Both of them recovered quickly and ran towards each other again. Now Matt held the bow like a longsword, swinging it around to strike Darion again. In the heat of fighting, Darion felt an echo of the pedjiaar's strength return to him. He was fearless now. This time, instead of just blocking the blow, he grabbed onto the bow tightly with both hands and twisted. Matt kept a firm hold, but Darion's strength and speed drew him off to one side, off balance again. Still holding the other end of the bow, Darion kicked out with his left leg and connected his boot with the inside of Matthien's thigh. Matt stayed upright but Darion heard him gasp in pain. He kicked again. And again. Each time Darion felt Matthien stagger for a moment. But then the older boy's greater strength began to count for something. He pushed Darion backwards towards the edge of the courtyard wall. There was an opening onto a flight of stone steps. These led down into a side alley set some distance below. Ignoring the pain, Matt forced the bow up between them, now using it to beat Darion in the chest as they crashed into the wall.

Darion felt himself growing weaker. The blood he had lost, dizzyness from so much effort and the pain of his wounds now all took their toll. His arms flailed helplessly as he tried to ward off Matthien's frenzy. He knew if he didn't get the upper hand in the next couple of moments, it would all be over for him.

Already he felt himself bent backwards by the force of Matthien's weight. The older boy had twisted them both away from the wall again and was forcing Darion to stumble backwards. They struggled nearer and nearer to the steep steps.

'I can't fight his extra weight,' Darion thought to himself. 'But I can use it against him.'

Grabbing the bow again with both hands, Darion allowed himself to be forced back and down towards the floor. As he did, he suddenly bent his knees, dropping fast, so that Matthien lurched forwards, caught off balance. Darion rolled onto his back and kicked upwards with both feet as Matthien started to fall on top of him. He made contact – hard – in the Variegatt lord's stomach and he heard a 'whuuff' of pain from his enemy's lips. Twisting the bow in his grip and pushing upwards with his legs once more he tipped Matthien head over heels onto the cobbles. Matt's head scraped heavily along the ground. He staggered up again, one side of his face now masked in blood.

Darion was already back on his feet. At last he had the upper hand. Matt's vision blurrred from the knock to his head. He squinted to see clearly through the blood stinging his eyes. Darion struck again. It was just a single blow only meant to knock him off his feet again, but now Matthien was standing too close to the edge of the stone steps. He tottered there for a moment, swinging his arms for balance like a particularly bad tightrope performer. Then he plunged down the stairs.

He tumbled out of Darion's sight. He heard a grunt and a sharp thudding crack from the bottom. Darion raced to look and there, contorted on the final few stairs, lay the body of Lord Matthien, young lord of the Variegatt. His head had twisted around on his neck in a way that reminded Darion of poor Vershan's twisted limbs. Darion knew immediately that his adversary was dead.

He couldn't leave the body here. It would be discovered in minutes. Up to now, if he had been challenged by a guard, there was a chance he could have made an excuse. People knew he had been a friend to Matthien, perhaps he could have talked his way out of trouble. He could even say that he was helping him to fight the ament who were attacking. But if he was caught during a search for the murderer of Lord Matthien, Darion knew no one would listen to him. He would never escape.

He would never be able to find Alianna.

He couldn't let that happen. He had to hide the body.

Darion raced down the steps. Trying to ignore the blood, Darion hauled the body up into his arms. He hoped that there would be a shadowy corner nearby; a place where Matthien's body would go unnoticed...at least for the time being. He knew that he should have been more upset, he should feel guilty about killing Matthien. But when he thought about Alianna lying in a pool of blood, when he thought about Vershan and about his mother being dragged away, he could feel nothing for the young man who had once pretended to be his friend.

A few metres away, on the opposite side of the alley, Darion noticed a wooden hatch in the ground. He recognised it as being one of the trapdoors through which barrels of ale, or sacks of grain and flour were delivered to the cellars of nearby shops and houses. Snatching up Matthien's bow once more, Darion ran across to the trapdoor. The lock holding the hatch closed looked old and rusty. It wouldn't take much effort to snap it open. He hooked one end of Matthien's bow through the padlock and gave it a rapid jerk upwards. Nothing. The lock creaked but stayed fastened. He tried again and this time the bow snapped in two. Darion hurled it away in frustration and looked around him. There were plenty of loose cobblestones nearby where an explosion had destroyed a low wall. He spotted one, a bit larger and heavier than most. He grabbed it. Kneeling down he hammered sideways at the old lock. With just the third attempt, it snapped open. Darion gave a silent cheer to himself and pulled open the trapdoors. He dropped the cobblestone down into the cellar and nodded his head in satisfaction as he counted a full second before he heard it clatter onto the floor in the darkness below.

He gave another hurried glance over his shoulder. Nobody up in the castle windows looking out. No one approaching from the gate or through the castle doorway. No shouts of alarm. So far his luck held. Now he just had to drag Matthien's body the last few metres to the trapdoor. *'Please,'* he begged to himself. *'Please, give me a few more moments.'*

He managed to haul the body across to the cellar opening and heaved it over the edge. Gravity took over and Matthien's body tumbled out of sight into the darkness below.

Darion didn't even wait to hear the crump of bones and flesh hitting the cellar floor. He threw the broken pieces of the bow down after their owner. Swinging the trapdoor closed he turned and ran towards the lair of his enemies once more.

Darion entered the building. Blood was still seeping from the wound in his side. He felt dizzy. If this went on he would soon be too weak to move. A torn flag hung down from one wall. He grabbed hold of it and pulled sharply. With a rip, a large piece of it came away in his hand. Darion looped the material tightly around his middle and knotted it as securely as he could to slow the bleeding. When he had finished, the torn ends of his improvised bandage hung down like a pirate's sash.

There were voices in the room ahead of him. He crept up and hid by the doorframe.

'We seem to have beaten back the ament for now.' It was Argolin's voice.

'The attack was unexpected, but we have shown our strength.' This time it was Gretton Tur who spoke. Darion felt his knees give way as he heard it. 'They have destroyed a few walls, caused us a little disturbance with their flares and fires, but they were never a real danger.'

So the explosions *had* come from within the city after all. Alianna had been right. It *was* the ament spies and their pulver guards who had attacked Argolin's men.

'Harrow must have gathered more evidence against us than we thought,' Argolin's voice went on. 'He must have ordered this attack.'

'Well we have shown them our power,' said Tur. 'They will think harder before they try again.'

'By then we will be ready. Your shifting is going ahead as planned?'

'Several are already transformed into brannoch,' Tur told him. 'But I have made them much larger and stronger this time and mixed them with the essences of dogs so they obey commands without question.'

'Are any more children available to shift?'

'As many as you like. Our guards can be on their way to the Tenementerra as soon as you command. There is no end to the wretches we can use.'

Darion thought he would be sick.

'What about the Melgardes whelp,' Tur continued. 'Any news of our striped pet?'

'My Jorian is still hunting for him as we speak. We needn't fear that little cur any longer. I saw the look in my boy's face as he set out to find him. He took Bargoth and Dross with him. He'll take his revenge on that boy very seriously. I promised him he could keep the pelt for a rug.'

Both men laughed. It was clear that Argolin didn't know about Jorian and his henchmen yet.

'And the girl?' asked Tur.

'That ament bitch? Escaped. Ran off towards the slum streets.'

Darion's head reeled. They were talking about Alianna. He had been right. She was alive after all!

'My guards reported sighting of a draccen,' Argolin continued. 'She was riding it with some other ament spy, a boy. Probably another of Harrow's gutter rats, like Melgardes. One of my men returned to say Matthien shot at them, bringing them down, but the boy escaped too.'

'And Matthien himself?'

'Ran off to chase the boy, he's sending back one of my men to report to me.'

The voices got lower. He thought that they must have turned away from him, or moved deeper into the room. Darion thought about what he had overheard. It was all good news! They did not know about Matthien yet and they still thought that he himself was probably dead, hunted and ready for skinning by Jorian. They wouldn't be looking for him. But the thing that thrilled him most was the news that Alianna had escaped.

They were still talking. He had to find out more information. Darion strained to hear.

He risked a look around the doorframe. If he could get a little bit closer he might be able to hear better. He could only make out parts of what Tur was saying as they moved around the room.

'…not tell the mother that her son is dead. We need some power over them so that…'

Then a snatch of Argolin's voice again.

'...there will be time to visit the dungeons later. Our prisoners down there can wait a little longer...'

'*The mother!*' Darion's head reeled. That could only mean one person. They were holding his mother down in the dungeons!

He remembered his conversation with Matthien during the party. How long ago that all seemed. '*And underneath the house are father's wine cellars. They used to be the dungeons.*' That was it. He had to find his way to the cellars. That must be where they were holding his mother. Suddenly he knew where to go. '*The kitchens,*' he said to himself. '*The doorway to the wine cellars must be in the kitchens.*'

*   *   *   *

The smoke had begun to thin by the time he reached the courtyard of Matthien's house. With a short look to left and right he quickened his pace to the oak doors. They were open. He plunged through.

There was no noise of fighting here. The corridors in this part of the building were deserted. Darion raced on, trying every door that he came to.

The smoke was still thick inside the building. The evening winds had not been able to clear it away here. It choked him as he ran.

He looked into the different rooms as he made his way through the building. All the time his ears strained to hear the sound of someone approaching, but downstairs at least the house seemed empty. The building was so big that after a couple of minutes he couldn't find his bearings in the twisting corridors. He forced himself to think. It was no use rushing on in a panic. He would only get himself lost.

He thought about the rooms he had already looked into. One had been a banqueting room, with a huge dining table in the middle. At the far end of that room he had seen another set of double doors. Wasn't it likely that the kitchens would be close to the dining hall? That the food would be brought straight from the ovens through those double doors? And wasn't it more than likely that the wine would be brought up from the cellars from the same place?

He raced back the way he had come. Rushing back into the dining hall he sped around the table and pushed at the doors. They swung open easily. He had been right, they led directly to the kitchens. Now, had he also been right about the entrance to the wine cellars?

Yes! Over to one side of the kitchen was an open doorway and Darion could see steps winding down beyond it. That had to be what he was looking for.

He ran towards the cellar doors and down the steps. They curved around in a spiral. Every fourteen or fifteen steps he came to a torch burning in the wall. They just about lit his way.

After descending several full turns, he came to a large cellar filled from floor to ceiling with wine racks and stacked bottles. Beyond it he saw a long corridor stretching ahead of him. Without pausing he set off.

He had to find his mother. He couldn't let her down. On he went through the darkness. He was deep down in the tunnels now. He must be getting closer to the cells. Two more minutes of moving forwards. Three minutes. Still no sign. No sound. Every thirty or forty paces his way was lit by another burning torch held by a chain to the corridor wall. The lights soon faded as he walked past them and he made several paces in near blackness before the next one began to light his way from up ahead.

Glancing around over his shoulder he considered the distance he had come. Two hundred paces? Three hundred? The building above him was huge, but it wasn't endless. How much further underground did these tunnels lead? He hadn't even seen a doorway or passage leading off to right or left. Was he going the wrong way? He noticed his breathing getting quicker. Darion told himself he mustn't start to panic. If he did, he wouldn't be able to think properly. He was sure to make a mistake. Slowing down his breath he tried to remain calm.

Soon though, he reached a stretch of corridor with no more lights. The darkness became deeper until every flicker of the last torch had disappeared around the corner behind him. He could hardly make out his own hand in front of his face. *'Must just be one of the torches that's burned out,'* he thought to himself. *'I must be coming the right way, they wouldn't have kept torches burning this far unless they were leading to something.'* He was sure that this reasoning made sense. It had to, otherwise he had no hope of finding his mother. Darion inched forwards. Every step took him an age. He daren't make the smallest sound. He wished he had the essence of a fruit fly, to enable him to move more swiftly and silently; or a cat, cats could see in the dark couldn't they? But all he had was himself. Himself and what *he* was.

He stumbled further on, feeling his way now along the wall. There was a stale, damp smell in his nose, and something else too; something worse; like old raw meat, going off.

Darion swallowed his disgust at the stink and carried on. His fingers were freezing and numb as they felt along the cold stone wall. Still nothing but darkness ahead of him. Had he missed a turning? Was he about to come to a dead end? Claustrophobic fear clutched at him as he thought about how far underground he must be. He breathed hard, trying not to let panic take over. The stench of the old flesh attacked his nostrils again. 'Just a few more paces,' he told himself. 'Then turn around and go back. Feel your way along the other wall this time, in case you missed a turning.'

But it was no good. Fear held him tighter with every step. What if he couldn't find his way back to the last torch? Why hadn't he thought to take one from the wall and bring it with him?

Just as he convinced himself that he had made a mistake, that he had no choice and he *had* to turn back, Darion saw another flicker of light up ahead. It threw a dim shadow on the cold stones ahead of him. Hardly bigger than the flare of a match. But this light carried on glowing. He strained his ears to catch any sound. There was nothing. He had to get closer.

Tiptoeing forwards, hardly breathing, Darion made his way towards the light.

Even Stranger Reunions

He heard whispering voices up ahead. Darion knew the first voice immediately. His mother! He had found her! Forgetting his caution now he hurried on. The floor was uneven. He tripped and stumbled onwards.

'Who's there?' The second voice hissed at him. It stopped him in his tracks. There was something familiar about this voice too. He fumbled forwards. There was another torch flickering on the wall. This was different to the others he had walked past earlier. It was only small, guttering and spluttering in the recesses of an alcove, but it was still enough for Darion to make his way.

Up ahead of him he could see a cell door. It was thick and solid, some sort of steel or iron. An opening had been carved into the metal half way up. The opening was barred with heavy iron rods. Inside he saw his mother. She held on to the bars and leant forwards, trying to see who was approaching. There was another figure just behind her, half in the shadows. Darion couldn't see this second figure clearly. Even so, he knew straight away who it was. A sob rose in his throat. It was a man with greying hair straggling down the sides of his face and tangling into a thick beard. He was thinner than Darion remembered, older and weaker than when he had last seen him. Even so there could be no mistaking who this was. Darion gulped air into his lungs and lurched forwards.

'Father!'

But this was impossible. His father was dead. He had been killed by Argolin's men. Except he hadn't. Here he was, not dead, but taken prisoner instead.

His father's arms were reaching out to him through the bars. 'My son, my son.' His words came in gasping breaths. In a moment Darion had hold of his parents' hands.

He could not find any words to say. His throat had closed up. He just looked at his father.

Finally he found his voice.

'Mother, did you...did you know?'

She shook her head. 'No Darion. Only when they took me and threw me down here.'

'At least they locked us up together,' his father said with a grim smile.

'Argolin's men wanted me to help them, Darion,' his father said. 'They threatened to put us all in danger, to take you and your mother. They told me that I would lose you both. They were desperate Darion. They threatened to kill you, or to take you away so I would never see you again. Well of course I believed them. I had seen their wickedness. I knew of their violence. They would not hesitate to do dreadful things.'

Darion thought about Vershan, the twisted limbs and burnt out body. He shuddered.

'I could not risk that,' his father said. 'I couldn't give them any reason, any opportunity to harm you or your mother.'

'So...*did* you...help them?' The thought that his father might have betrayed the people of Beltheron was too much for him to bear. 'To stop them hurting us?'

'I made them think that,' his father said. 'But all of the information I gave to Argolin came through Harrow himself. We fed him false information and at the same time, tried to discover the extent of Argolin's own treachery.' He placed his hand on his wife's shoulder. 'Your mother knew nothing of this. I could not burden her with the fear that we were all living on such a knife edge. She needed to be able to carry on as normal as if nothing strange was going on. I knew that we were being watched by Argolin's spies and I could give them no reason to become suspicious.'

'What they were doing was terrible Darion,' his mother continued.

He nodded. 'I know.'

'The Select families and some of the other lords were close to a deal with the Maraglar merchants,' his father went on. 'It would have meant peace for our city. However Argolin feared he would lose his position of influence, his power to trade and deal with them. Argolin didn't want peace. He wanted the threat of war to give him a reason to take even more control over the city and eventually seize control of Maraglar too.'

'Harrow started to tell me,' Darion said. 'And about Gretton Tur as well.'

His father spat out his disgust at the mention of Tur. 'That creature cares only for potions. He wants to manipulate, control and experiment for his own fascination and satisfaction. Argolin gave him the means to do it.'

Darion spoke up again, nodding enthusiastically, pleased to be able to offer his father new information. 'He took young people from our streets and used them for terrible experiments. They're making an army of shape shifters, brannoch and worse, to fight for them.' Darion paused. He didn't know how to tell them the rest. 'He, Gretton Tur I mean...he experimented on me, he turned me into...'

His mother gasped in shock. She reached out through the bars towards him.

'Oh my boy, my poor boy.'

His father's face was set in fury.

'There'll be time to talk of all this later,' he said. 'But right now we need to get out. Son, can you help us?'

Darion looked at the bars of the cell door. There were three bolts securing it into the wall. Each one was as thick as his wrist. They were fastened in place by three huge padlocks. These were old and rusty, but one look at them told Darion he would never be able to break them. He grabbed hold of one and it was a so heavy that he could hardly even move it against the door. He let it drop back with a thud.

He looked around. Was there some sort of tool he could use? There was nothing he could see. Darion ran to the alcove and took down the torch. Close up, the heat made him flinch back. He felt it begin to scorch his fingers and adjusted his grip to hold it lower down.

Moving the light from side to side in front of him, he continued to search.

Neither of his parents spoke. Both just nodded encouragement at him. He could see the pride in his father's eyes and a new respect from his mother. He felt a lump in his throat. He could do this, he *would* do it. He *had* to. Turning back down the corridor, Darion searched around for something strong enough to break open the heavy lock.

He didn't have to go far. Several of the stones used to build the walls of the tunnels had crumbled away. There were plenty of large pieces to choose from. Darion picked up one of the heaviest and made his way back to his parents' cell.

'Stand back.'

Holding the stone in both hands he pounded at the first lock. It resisted his first few blows, but then, with a snap, he felt the metal buckle. His mother stepped forwards and helped him to twist the broken metal apart. The second padlock was harder work and he scuffed his knuckles against the bars several times before it broke open. The last one however, was easy. Just one hard blow from the stone and it crumbled into rusting pieces. His father pushed at the barred door and in another moment his parents were hugging him tightly.

'My son, my son,' his father breathed. 'I have hoped for this for so long.'

Darion's throat had closed up and he knew if he tried to talk he would burst into tears.

Together they turned and made their way back though the corridors under the castle.

Retribution

It didn't seem to take as long to return to the kitchens. Darion and his parents crept cautiously through to the dining room, alert to any sound. But all was silent.

'*Maybe the battle is over,*' thought Darion. '*Perhaps we've missed the rest of it.*'

He didn't believe it though. He kept thinking about Tur's terrifying words: '*There are plenty of children in the Tenementerra.*' His plans weren't over yet. Tur meant to shift as many young people as he could. Darion couldn't let him get away with that.

'We have to get back to our part of the city,' he said to his mother and father. 'There might still be time to warn some of the families.'

His father nodded his agreement. They headed for the main doors and ran out into the courtyard. The three of them reached the bottom of the staricase and started to run across the cobbles. Then they heard a harsh voice behind them.

'Stop right there!'

Darion spun around. Standing at the top of the steps was Argolin. Bargoth and Dross were on either side. Darion's father gave a strangled cry of anger and began running back towards the High Lord. He brandished a sword he had taken from the hall on their way out.

Darion felt his mother's hand on his shoulder. Both watched as his father got closer to Argolin.

The High Lord grinned. With a simple twist of his hand he released his own sword from its scabbard.

'Come on then, ament trash,' he said. 'I have waited long enough for this.'

With a single cry, Darion leapt forwards to help his father. His mother screamed out to stop him but it was too late. He was already half way across the courtyard.

Bargoth and Dross had also drawn their swords. They ran towards Darion.

Argolin and his father clashed first. Their weapons rang out with fury.

Suddenly, high up above them they heard a shriek. Darion looked up and saw three grey draccen swooping down through the cloud. A flash of lightning lit up the sky for a second. He saw the green livery of the draccen riders. Darion remembered the party in the great hall. The representatives from Maraglar wore green livery. It was them! Maraglar agents! They were coming for their meeting with Argolin.

They shot closer, and now Darion saw their outstretched arms. They held long staves pointing towards his father. Fire crackled from the tip of one and Darion felt the jolt shudder through his feet as a flaming bolt hit the ground of the courtyard.

'Father, look out!' Darion's cry came too late as a second bolt of fire struck closer to his father, knocking him to his knees.

But then there came another screeching cry. High above them all flew Carccen Firetongue. She screeched again and dipped her wings, swooping down towards the three dark draccen of Maraglar.

Darion glanced up. Carccen wasn't alone. There was someone riding between her shoulder blades. He saw a billowing wave of chestnut hair and then a familiar face searching the ground below.

Alianna.

A cheer leapt up in his heart as he saw her.

He heard a shout of anger, another of alarm from above his head. The draccen swooped down so their riders could get closer to the battle raging below them. Smoke still billowed from broken windows. Stone and broken rubble from shattered walls spilled into the courtyards of the great houses of the Variegatt.

Carccen was joined by another draccen now. Darker, like a deep blue midnight sky, and huge. Its wingspan dwarfed that of Carccen and the three draccen from Maraglar. Giving a piercing cry it swept down to the battle. There was no mistaking the figure riding her. Cleve Harrow's robes swirled around him as fire flashed from his hand.

The Maraglar pulled the reins steering their own beasts. The three grey draccen spun around, long necks coiling. Hissing savagely they streamed towards Harrow and Alianna.

Darion held his breath, eyes fixed on Alianna. Her hand shot out and a burst of flame crackled from her fingers. He remembered seeing her do this on the day the brannoch had attached the classroom. He hadn't had time to think about it then, but now he knew of course, that she had been trained by Harrow. She had mastered his ament skills in magic and fighting.

The men from Maraglar looked from one side to another in their confusion. As the draccen flew around each other Darion heard their angry, frightened voices. One of them pointed down to the fighting on the ground below and gestured at the smoking Variegatt and crumbled buildings.

Darion did not understand the Maraglar words, but their frustrated meaning was clear: '*This is no place to stay! See the danger here? These fools fight amongst themselves.*

*There's no profit in remaining here.'

In the same moment they all pulled on their reins. The grey draccen coiled away from Carccen Firetongue and up into the sky. Harrow's mighty steed pursued them, her wings flapping steadily as they disappeared into the clouds.

Darion's attention turned back to the battle on the ground. Bargoth and Dross had fled at the first sight of the draccen. His father stood in the middle of the courtyard. He leant heavily on his sword, gasping for breath. A deep gash ran the length of his face, from eyebrow to chin. Despite this, his father was grinning fiercely. At his feet, scorched by the stray flames of the fighting draccens' breath, lay the body of Argolin.

Within moments, Carccen landed Alianna on the ground. Darion could see the gash on her forehead, deep with thickened, drying blood. Otherwise she seemed unharmed. Whatever missile had struck her to the ground earlier, it did not seem to have caused any further damage.

She raced over to them, disbelief in her face at the sight of his father.

'You're alive?'

'It seems so lass.' She grabbed hold of him and hugged him tightly. He looked down at Argolin. 'More than can be said for this vermin.'

'Is he...?'

Darion's father nodded. 'Yes, Ali, he's dead.'

Darion heard the way his father shortened Alianna's name. He saw the affection in their eyes for each other. It was bizarre to think that they knew each other so well.

Alianna turned towards him.

'Darry, are you alright?'

He nodded, 'I think so.'

She grinned and ran over to hug him. 'It's over Darry. Argolin's dead. And our pulver will soon round up the rest of his soldiers.'

Another thought suddenly occurred to him. 'Gretton Tur! What about him?'

She was about to reply when there was a cry from overhead. They all looked up. Harrow was sweeping back down on the back of the mighty dark blue draccen. It landed in the wrecked courtyard sending up a cloud of grey dust. Carccen gave a cry of welcome and the two draccen curled their necks together in friendship. Harrow climbed down to greet them.

He saw Darion's father and his face creased in delight.

'Targen! This is a happy day indeed.'

The two men embraced as Harrow's aments came running from the great hall.

Harrow turned to speak to them. 'Any news of Tur?' he asked.

They shook their heads. 'Cannot be found, Cleve. But the door to his rooms is locked and their seems nothing we can do to open it.'

'It's as though it is barred by some spell or other.'

Harrow looked grim. 'I have my own spells and ways of opening doors without need of a key.' He turned to one of the ament. 'Keep watch here over the body of this disgraced man,' he gestured to Argolin's corpse. 'We will go in search of Tur...if indeed he is to be found anywhere.'

They set off together; Harrow, Ali, Darion, his mother and father and the rest of the ament agents, through the streets and back to the college buildings. On their way they saw that no damage had been done to the rest of the city. The pulver attacking Argolin and his Guild had contained the fighting in that one small group of streets and buildings in the Variegatt. Even so, there were many throughout the Cittegarre who came out of their houses to look at this strange motley of people, dusty, limping and battle scarred, as they made their way through the city.

Up ahead, they saw two familiar figures skulking near to a door to the college courtyard.

'Dross! Bargoth!' cried Alianna.

The two villains had been fumbling with small vials of liquid when they heard her voice. Looking up at their pursuers, both men now lifted the small bottles to their lips and drank.

In an instant, a low rumbling sound began. The earth shook beneath them. Before any of them could do anything, a blinding column of white light shot up from the ground at the feet of Bargoth and Dross.

Everyone shielded their eyes and when they next looked, the light had faded to a low, reddish glow and the two men had disappeared.

Harrow raced towards the spot by the door. Everyone else rushed after him. The Cleve looked down and Darion saw his shoulders slump in dismay and defeat.

The others all followed his gaze. There on the ground where Bargoth and Dross had been standing, were two dark scorch marks burnt deep into the earth.

'They have gone,' he said. 'Tur has released some old magic indeed. He has opened up a pathway for them to escape.'

'But where?' asked Darion.

'That I do not know. Come, let us go in.'

When they finally crossed the courtyard and climbed to Tur's rooms they saw the door was now open.

'But this is not how we left this place,' the first ament pulver cried. 'The door was locked tight not an hour ago.'

'Then Gretton Tur has obviously returned since, and in a great hurry,' said Harrow. 'My guess is that he needed some potion, some spell or equipment from here, to help him escape.' Harrow paused for a moment. 'If I am right,' he murmured to himself. 'Then that is how he helped those two villains to disappear a few moments ago.'

He nodded to himself, thinking deeply. 'Yes, that would be a way for him to go somewhere where he could never be found.'

They all watched him intently.

'Wait here,' said Harrow. He stepped forwards and through the open doorway.

Darion and Alianna looked at each other. He saw her eyes were filled with tension again. His hand reached for hers and he felt her grasp it tightly.

They all waited for a couple of minutes. It seemed like an hour to Darion. Then Harrow reappeared in the doorframe.

'You can come in now,' he said. 'Tur is not here anymore. It is as I feared. He has escaped somewhere, but I am not sure where, or indeed how.'

'What do you mean Cleve?' his father asked.

'See for yourselves.' Harrow stepped back and gestured with his arm for them to enter.

Darion's mouth dropped open when he saw the wreckage of Tur's chambers. Books and boxes and been ripped from the shelves, many jars and bottles were missing from their places and from what he could tell, bundles of documents had been burnt in the fireplace in one corner. It was still smoking and charred from the blackened packages of paper smouldering in the grate.

'It seems he tried to cover his tracks and destroy the information about his experiments,' said Harrow.

He led them all through the tapestried doorway into the room beyond. The room where Tur conducted his tortures and experiments. Darion swallowed hard as he stepped through the tapestry, but he felt Alianna's hand, still squeezing his, and this made everything easier.

Harrow was standing in the middle of the room. They all gathered around him.

'But where has Tur gone?' Darion asked.

'That I cannot tell you,' said Harrow. 'But I can show you where he went *from*.'

He pointed down to a place on the floor by his feet.

There, on the flagstones in the middle of Tur's room, was a dark scorch mark burnt deep into the earth.

Epilogue

The animal on the table skips about happily. Its foot pulls at a piece of string. The string runs across the full length of the table and down to the floor where it is tied to a lever. The creature's foot pulls again and the lever releases a small trapdoor. A fat, tasty nut drops onto the creature's feeding tray. The animal hops down and pecks happily at the nut with its large beak. A man reaches forwards and gently strokes its feathery head.

'Creena wins again. Creena's smart,' it says.

A second figure steps out of the shadows at the edge of the room. He has watched everything.

'Still experimenting then?' he says.

The first man smiles. 'No, Darion. This is just a game that Creena and I like to play.'

Darion nods briefly. He turns away from the bird and from his teacher, and walks over to the window.

There is a long silence between them.

'The struggle isn't over yet, you know,' says Cleve Harrow. 'I know.'

'There are still followers of Argolin to deal with. Pulver soldiers who are still loyal to him. They meet in secret. They are plotting.'

'And what am I expected to do about that?' Darion is still staring out of the window.

'You have showed bravery before. I don't doubt that, if faced with more dangers, you will do so again.'

Darion isn't so sure. He thinks he might have had enough of bravery and danger.

Harrow presses on. 'The Maraglar have gone. They have no more interest in our city, for now. But one day they might have ambitions for Beltheron once more.'

'I can't see how I could be of any help with that either.'

'You aren't the same young lad who first walked into my classroom.'

Darion can't look at Harrow. He just stares at the ground.

'Alianna started in the same way you did. A little younger than you are now perhaps, maybe a little more dedicated, but no more talented than you.'

Darion keeps his gaze glued to the same place down by his feet.

'And you have been through lessons, experiences which she has never had.'

'Huh, you don't have to remind me.'

He thinks about some of those lessons.

He thinks about Vershan, a true friend. If he were still here then he would know how to deal with all of this. Vershan always knew what to do.

'You were just a clumsy young student when I first met you,' says Harrow.

This is true. He had been clumsy, and scared, and often selfish.

'I *used* to be like that.'

'But now, Darion?' says Harrow. 'If you feel differently now, and I think you do, then I have a role for you to play. A job for you to do.' He walks towards the door. He pauses and looks back. 'Your father believes you do too. And so does Alianna.' Harrow turns and walks through the door, leaving it open behind him.

He still feels uncertain. But Harrow is right. He knows he feels different now to that clumsy frightened young boy. Something essential has changed in him.

He gently ruffles Creena's feathers. She gives a contented squawk. Darion smiles. He turns and walks through the door, following Cleve Harrow out of his study.

The End

You can read more of the adventures of
Cleve Harrow, Gretton Tur, and the world
of Beltheron in

The Beltheron Sequence

The Beltheron Pathway, The Beltheron Select,
The Beltheron Darkness

By Chris Connaughton

All available to buy at
www.intextperformance.com